Cast of Charac

Emily Murdock. Proprietor of the Lent[ ]
first husband wasn't a bad sort but he [ ]
doesn't mind paint but so far he's ignore[ ]

Henry Bryce. He works for Emily and lives in an apartment connected to the shop. He's fond of Emily but after his first wife threw hot coffee in his face he isn't so sure he wants to try marriage again.

Lincoln "Link" Simpson. His antique shop is located on the floor beneath Emily's. He asks Emily to marry him at least twice a year.

Cornelia Lord. Henry's sister. She's tried suicide a few times but it never took. Henry says she wants the universe wrapped up in cellophane and delivered by a postman who never heard of C.O.D. She doesn't want Henry to marry Emily.

James "Beansie" Lord. Cornelia's husband. Henry can't figure out why a nice, orderly, kindly fellow like him would marry his sister. James has recently been swindled in a deal in Las Vegas.

Cleo Delaphine. She's a newly divorced, unpleasant sort of woman who bribes Emily and was also involved in the Las Vegas deal. She isn't around long.

Dr. Harmon Delaphine. Her ex-husband. Everyone agrees he's a swell guy.

Beardsley and Martha Satchel. A quarreling couple, they live above Henry and have convinced him that he's right to avoid marriage.

Mrs. Albert Giddings. The Daniel Webster bust belongs to her, though she left it at Emily's shop more than a year ago. She also lost money in the Las Vegas scam.

Percy Ford, Jr. A "colorless, odorless, and tasteless man" who lived across the street from Emily's shop in the Thinker's Club but who died in a most inconvenient spot.

Donald Clark. A mystery man.

Plus **Roscoe,** who also works for Emily (and adores her); **Clarence Mould,** a theatrical producer who tried to borrow the bust; **Mr. Gottlieb,** who runs the nearby deli; **Joe Cassamassima,** a furrier of questionable ethics; **Hilda Leghorn,** Emily's sharp-tongued hairdresser friend; and **McNulty** and **Burgreen,** two of New York's finest.

Books by Margaret Scherf

Featuring Emily and Henry Bryce
The Gun in Daniel Webster's Bust (1949)
The Green Plaid Pants (1951)
Glass on the Stairs (1954)
The Diplomat and the Gold Piano (1963)

Featuring the Reverend Martin Buell
Always Murder a Friend (1948)
Gilbert's Last Toothache (1949)
The Curious Custard Pie (1950)
The Elk and the Evidence (1952)
The Cautious Overshoes (1956)
Never Turn Your Back (1959)
The Corpse in the Flannel Nightgown (1965)

Featuring Grace Severance
The Banker's Bones (1968)
The Beautiful Birthday Cake (1971)
To Cache a Millionaire (1972)
The Beaded Banana (1978)

Featuring Lieutenant Ryan
The Owl in the Cellar (1945)
Murder Makes Me Nervous (1948)

Nonseries
The Corpse Grows a Beard (1940)
The Case of the Kippered Corpse (1941)
They Came to Kill (1942)
Dead: Senate Office Building (1953)
Judicial Body (1957)
If You Want Murder Well Done (1974)
Don't Wake Me Up While I'm Driving (1977)

For Children
The Mystery of the Velvet Box (1963)
The Mystery of the Empty Trunk (1964)
The Mystery of the Shaky Staircase (1965)

Historical Novel
Wedding Train (1960)

The Gun in Daniel Webster's Bust

by Margaret Scherf

Introduction by
Tom & Enid Schantz

Rue Morgue Press
Lyons / Boulder

The Rue Morgue Press
P.O. Box 4119
Boulder, Colorado 80306
800-699-6214
www.ruemorguepress.com

Printed by
Johnson Printing

PRINTED IN THE UNITED STATES OF AMERICA

Margaret Scherf's account of the woes of being a mystery writer is taken from a
piece reprinted in *The Doubleday Crime Club Compendium 1928-1991*, edited by
Ellen Nehr. The editor does not cite where the piece originally appeared.

About Margaret Scherf

VERY EARLY on in her writing career Margaret Scherf made it clear that readers wishing for serious or weighty topics would do better to look elsewhere. Even the titles of her first two books, *The Corpse Grows a Beard* (1940) and *The Case of the Kippered Corpse* (1941) are—well, dead giveaways of her intent to amuse rather than to thrill or scare the pants of her readers. Of course, that didn't stop fans and friends from trying to persuade her to be a tad more literary. But Margaret—Peggy to everyone but the reading public—wasn't about to change, sticking her tongue firmly in cheek and offering up the following explanation:

It is very difficult to be a writer. If you are a dentist, your friends accept the fact and let your profession alone more or less. But if you are one kind of writer, people are always trying to make you into some other kind of writer. Especially if you happen to write mysteries. This is looked upon as easier than but in the same class as strip tease. 'When are you going to write something really serious?' they ask. Of course they know I haven't an idea in my head and they would read anything serious with my name on it. What drove me to writing was that nobody would listen to me talk.

People who can't pick up their offices and move them to Montana or Italy when they feel like it become very irritated when they see someone else doing it. Particularly New Yorkers. They think a little poverty would be salutary, so they try to needle me into doing something they know that I can't do. Instead of cheerfully knocking off people in pleasant surroundings, they want me to take death seriously. "We have Shakespeare and Tennessee Williams," I remind them. "Isn't there room for one lightweight?"

They answer me with, "Why don't you write about love?" Frankly I don't feel that I know enough about biology. Love has become so intimately anatomical in today's fiction that I'm afraid to tackle it.

I have made concessions to critics, though. My aunt said that there was too much whiskey in my books, so I did one with nothing but Coca-Cola. And my father objected to that; he dislikes Coca-Cola as fiercely as he does the French parliament. You can't please everybody.

In addition to your friends, you have to think sometimes about your readers. Something told me to go to England last fall, and when I was settled in Sheriff's Hotel in Bath I was up to my ears in material for murder. Two delicious old ladies gave off wonderful dialogue over their breakfast kipper. The ceiling in the dining room flaked and fell into the food (mix arsenic or cyanide with plaster that there might be a story in that); there were gloomy subcellars, and a cistern that was just the place to dispose of several bodies.

Detective Inspector Coles at the Bath Police Station gave me all the data on procedure including: *Means of Identifying Bodies Found in Cisterns* and *How to Test Plaster for Traces of Arsenic and Cyanide*. I was all set. I came home and told Crime Club editor Isabelle Taylor that I proposed to do a story with an English setting.

I crossed the ocean, lived in England for four months, did all that research and what happens? My editor informed me gently that she has quite enough English corpses in stock, and added that Americans prefer to have American mystery writers kill off American corpses in American locales.

And so I'm left with nothing to show for four months' research in England but the information that the local police and Scotland Yard are not rivals. But I don't see how I'm going to use it in a mystery story set in Montana.

Even with all those difficulties, however, it is very rewarding to be a writer because of the awe and reverence with which people regard this profession. The questions they ask make this obvious. The one I hear most often is: "Are you working now or are you still writing?"

Even though she didn't take herself seriously, Scherf was as serious about her writing as she was about the other great passions in her life:

travel, Montana, antiques and Democratic party politics. Scherf was born on April Fools Day 1908 in Fairmont, West Virginia, a largish town in the northern part of the state near Morgantown and the Pennsylvania border. Her father was a high school teacher and the family moved first to New Jersey and then to Wyoming, before finally settling in Montana. After graduation from high school in Cascade, Montana, she attended Antioch College (1925-1928) in Yellow Springs, Ohio, a very small town near Dayton. She left college short of graduation to take a job as an editorial secretary with Robert M. McBride, a book publishing firm located in New York City. Wanderlust struck her in 1929 and she embarked on a round-the-world trip, an experience that would instill in her a love of travel that would stay with her for the rest of her life. Upon her return to the United States, she joined the staff of the Camp Fire Girls national magazine in 1932 (an experience she would put to use in 1948's *Murder Makes Me Nervous*), then moved on to the staff of the Wise Book Company as a secretary and copywriter in 1934. In 1939, she quit her job and launched her career as a full-time writer, publishing three mysteries with Putnam between 1940 and 1942. With the advent of World War II, she temporarily abandoned her writing career and took a job as Secretary to the Naval Inspector, Bethehem Steel Shipyard in Brooklyn.

After the war, she returned to writing and eventually found herself back in Montana, a state she was to call home for the rest of her life. She had enjoyed her years in New York but she much preferred life in small towns. She continued to revisit New York settings in her books during this period, most notably in the Emily and Henry Bryce series, but her postwar books were primarily set in more rustic locales. "Small town characters, especially Episcopalians, were my delight," she wrote to a critic in 1979.

Chief among those characters was the Reverend Martin Buell, an Episcopalian minister just on the wrong side of middle age who brings both his housekeeper and a "we'll do things my way" attitude to a small Montana parish (the original Doubleday Crime Club edition preface mistakenly said the series was set in Colorado, presumably because Easterners think mountains exist only in the Mile High State). Martin's bishop explained that things had been "slipping" in the parish and the parishioners needed a bit of "bullying." He sent the right man. Buell was to ride roughshod over his parishioners during the course of seven books published between 1948 and 1965.

Scherf alternated the Buell books with a daffy series featuring Emily and Henry Bryce, two Manhattan decorators. When we first meet them in 1949's *The Gun in Daniel Webster's Bust*, Emily is pushing Henry to marry him, an idea that doesn't sit too well with him given the fact his last marriage ended when his wife threw a cup of hot coffee in his face. But marry they did, and continued to solve crimes in their own fashion, Emily providing the right-brained, intuitive approach to crime solving while the left-brained Henry relied—more or less—on logic. The Bryce series ended in 1963 after four books.

Her other major series featured Dr. Grace Severance, a retired pathologist. This series, like Scherf herself, moved between Montana and Arizona, beginning with Arizona-based *The Banker's Bones* in 1968 and ending four books later in 1978 with *The Beaded Banana,* set in Montana. The Arizona locale was a familiar one by this time, as Scherf was now spending her winters in Quartzsite, Arizona, a small mining town near the California border, halfway between Phoenix and Las Vegas, Nevada

But she was no longer alone. In 1965, at the age of 57, she shocked friends and relatives by marrying Perry E. Beebe. Her relatives shook their heads with amusement at this December bride but later admitted that married life seemed to suit her just fine. She helped her husband run a cherry orchard near Yellow Bay, Montana, when she wasn't writing or tending to one of the three antique shops she owned at various times in and around Kalispell. The same year she married Perry the politically outspoken Scherf was also elected as a Democrat to the Montana state legislature. Scherf later gave a lighthearted account of her days as a politician in an article entitled "One Cow, One Vote." Perry died in 1975 and Peggy moved into a house she had built in Bigfork. On May 12, 1979, she was struck and killed by a drunk driver south of Kalispell.

Scherf's career began near the end of the Golden Age of detective fiction but, unlike those of so many other contemporary female authors, her career didn't decline in the early 1950s when the rental libraries disappeared and the market came to be dominated by male-oriented paperback originals. More than half of her books were published after the watershed year of 1953. Apparently there was still a good market for a writer who didn't take herself seriously but was serious about writing funny books.

Tom & Enid Schantz
December 2004
Lyons, Colorado

Chapter 1

Mrs. Delaphine replaced the gilded telephone. She was smiling. She felt completely confident that the scheme would work, and without too much unpleasant discussion. She stretched her arms above her head and the pale blue silk of her wide sleeves rippled to her shoulders. She looked at herself approvingly in the glass wall. It would be wonderful to have money again, enough money. She could toss Harmon's miserable alimony to cab drivers and waiters in tips if she wanted to.

She turned slowly, examining the room for things she wanted changed. She would have the blue niches redone in gold, and then buy the girandoles in Lincoln Simpson's shop. Miss Murdock would do the niches beautifully, if one could only pin her down to a day and an hour. The poor thing had no sense of time—completely irresponsible. But there must be some way—perhaps she could be bribed or flattered. Mr. Simpson would know—he was friendly with Miss Murdock and that Mr. Bryce. Rather amusing, Mr. Bryce. Dreadful neckties.

Mrs. Delaphine dressed with great care, calculating the effect of each garment and each piece of jewelry. Too bad she couldn't wear the mink, but it had to be out of circulation for a while. Meanwhile she had the black broadtail. When she dressed she usually thought of Cornelia Lord, as if Cornelia were standing there and looking her over with those

9

hostile cold eyes. Sometimes she was actually afraid of Cornelia. If Cornelia said you looked well, you could be sure you looked superlatively well.

She called to the maid who was cleaning the bathroom, picked up the mink cape, and let herself out. The heavy perfume she had used protected her from the unexpected odors of East Sixty-second Street. In the street she turned and looked up at her house. She still liked the turquoise-blue stucco with the sand-pink iron balcony—it did look superior to anything else in the block, particularly the converted brownstone next door with the usual red door and blue-tiled entrance. Mr. Bryce lived there, and Miss Murdock was in that rather new apartment building across the street. Odd how you could live in the same street with people and yet be on an entirely different social level.

She walked to the corner of Sixty-second and Lexington Avenue. An idea occurred to her. Miss Murdock would be flattered by an invitation to lunch at the Colony. Why not ask her, and in that way get her to the apartment? She could do the work on the niches in an hour, and meanwhile one could dangle the lunch in front of her as one leads on a donkey with hay. Of course such an invitation might lead to a mistaken feeling of equality and intimacy on the part of Miss Murdock. But one could take care of that when the need arose. There were ways of extricating oneself.

Mrs. Delaphine made her way along the avenue to the shop of Cassamassima the furrier. The little man smiled and bowed from behind his counter. "Yes, Mrs. Delaphine," he lisped.

"I want this cape glazed."

"Yes?" He reached for it, gave it a quick summary with his hard little eyes. "You think it needs glazing, Mrs. Delaphine? I never refuse work, don't misunderstand me, but this cape—it is in beautiful condition. Like new."

"I said I wanted it glazed, Mr. Cassamassima." She returned his stare.

"Certainly, certainly," he said, instantly making out a ticket.

"And don't lose it."

"A mink cape?" He smiled. "We don't lose no mink capes here, ma'am."

She accepted the receipt. "Completely illegible," she remarked. "You ought to learn to write, Mr. Cassamassima."

Mrs. Delaphine crossed the street to Link Simpson's antique shop. The girandoles were still in the window. She went down the two steps into the store and found Mr. Simpson rubbing off a suit of armor. His smile, she felt, was cool. She liked tradespeople to be a little more cordial, a little more anxious to please.

"Well, Mr. Simpson," she asked crisply, "how much are they today?"

"The girandoles?" He went on rubbing the foolish shoulder piece with a dirty yellow cloth. "Same price."

"Oh, come now. You didn't pay more than thirty dollars for the pair. I know you dealers. I'll give you fifty dollars, not a cent more."

He shook his head. "Sorry."

Mrs. Delaphine felt a disturbing irritation. She wanted to enjoy her purchase—she loved spending money—but Mr. Simpson was making it difficult. "Let's not quarrel," she persuaded. "I'll give you a hundred and twenty-five."

Mr. Simpson put down the rag. "That's fair," he said. "But I'm afraid I'll have to ask you to settle that other small bill before I can deliver the girandoles."

This was more than irritating, it was insulting. "Do you mean you question my ability to pay for these ridiculous things?"

He gave her a weary frown. "No, Mrs. Delaphine. I know you can pay. But I'm a small operator. I don't have great resources, and I can't afford to wait a year for my money."

"Oh, nonsense. It can't be that long since I took the chairs!"

He flipped through a card file. "December ninth a year ago. As this is December twelfth, I believe that makes it a year and three days."

"I hate people to be small about money," she said. "But I'll humor you, Mr. Simpson. I'll give you a check now. How's that?"

"For the whole thing?" he inquired.

"The whole thing. And I want the girandoles immediately. They'll have to be cleaned, of course. And you must replace the broken drops."

"I can't replace them today, Mrs. Delaphine. It takes time to find those crystals. If you want them to match."

"You can find them today. Be businesslike, Mr. Simpson, you'll get along better." She gave him a wide smile, forcing one from him, but she had the feeling that he didn't like her. Oh well, you simply couldn't make some people like you. "I'm going upstairs to see Miss Murdock now. I'm going to bribe her—if she'll do the niches immediately I'm going to take her to lunch at the Colony. Isn't that a clever idea?"

"Very," he said shortly. "I'm sure Miss Murdock will be deeply flattered."

"I thought so too." She replaced her checkbook. "You'll deliver the
girandoles tomorrow afternoon at the latest, won't you, Mr. Simpson?"

"I don't see how I can."

"But I simply must have them—it's for a party. Please?"

He shrugged. "I'll do my best."

She left the shop and opened the door at the bottom of the stairway
which led to the studio of the Lentement Decorating Company. Mrs.
Delaphine, on the last day but one of her existence, was completely
herself.

Upstairs in the studio Henry Bryce was putting a gold stripe on a
potbellied chest of drawers. He stopped for a moment to light a
cigarette, looked down on Lexington Avenue where a girl with a
nice pair of legs was being yanked along by a Bedlington on a leash.
The girl passed out of his line of vision and he raised his eyes to the
windows of the Thinkers' Club. A small round man with pink ears
and a luminous pink scalp stood in one long window and looked
down at the street as Henry had been doing. One could see quite
plainly into the lounge in back of him on a dark day like this, and the
polished walnut, the deep chairs, the soft, melon-colored lights were
in disdainful contrast to conditions in the studio—it took a cold-
sober person to make his way from the metal fire door at the front
of the shop to the plumbing accommodations in the rear without
falling over a plaster lady wearing a rose, a dismembered clock, a
crystal sconce, a can of paint, or a customer.

"You're sniffling, Henry," Emily accused. "Have you a cold?"

"I don't know."

"You'd better take something. Roscoe, close the window. Henry thinks
he has a cold."

Roscoe closed the window and went on making a brown grandfather's
clock pea green. Roscoe did easy, plain work as some of his marbles,
according to Emily, were square.

The phone rang and Henry picked up the paint-encrusted receiver. It
was Link Simpson. "Mrs. Delaphine is on her way up to work a scheme
on Emily," he said. "Watch out. She's in a queenly mood."

"Okay, thanks. We'll have the extinguishers ready." He hung up and turned to Emily, but before he could say anything Mrs. Delaphine came in. Henry hadn't seen her for several months, not since her divorce from Dr. Harmon Delaphine. Before that they had done a good deal of work for her because Harmon thought it might help to straighten out the kinks in her gnarled personality. Harmon was a good guy, patient and kindly, and for his sake they had put up with his wife. Henry didn't see why they should bother with her now, particularly as she was supposed to be rather slow pay since the divorce.

Thinking these things, he turned on a smile and cleared a chair for Mrs. Delaphine.

"Oh, let me look around," she bubbled, "it's been such a long time."

"Don't get lost. Things are pretty thick in here just now," Henry warned, looking her over. Her face was smooth under several layers of special "over-forty" cream, her lipstick was blotted to a genteel pink, her hair had come through various trial colors and emerged a reddish blond, very well done.

She wandered down the narrow aisle between the tiers of strange objects awaiting Emily's gifted paintbrush. "People do have the most dreadful things, don't they?" she exclaimed. "Who needs two gold eagles on a pedestal? Good heavens, don't tell me this is Mrs. Giddings' plaster bust? You had that when I used to come here!"

"Oh, I don't think so," Emily said, winking at Henry. "It must have been another one."

"This is Webster, isn't it?" Mrs. Delaphine insisted. "I'm sure it's the same—you used to joke about it."

"We'll get to it one of these days," Henry told her. "Meanwhile, Mrs. Giddings isn't in any great need of it."

Mrs. Delaphine laughed and said it was wonderful to have such a casual attitude.

"I wonder if Mrs. Giddings is still alive?" Emily asked hopefully.

"Of course she's alive—I saw her last week." Mrs. Delaphine came back to the windows. "Miss Murdock, I have a wonderful idea."

Henry thought, "Here it comes," but there was no way to warn Emily, who stood there with her trustful smile, her mouth slightly open.

"How would you like to have lunch with me at the Colony?"

"Oh." Emily's eyes got round. "When?"

"Tomorrow, say about half-past one? You could come over to the apartment a little earlier—and maybe you'd be sweet enough to dab some gold paint on those niches in my living room? It wouldn't take you a minute, I know, you're so quick and clever."

Henry interrupted. "We're terribly busy, Mrs. Delaphine. Miss Murdock would like to do you a favor, but we really can't afford the time just now. Christmas is our busiest season—everyone wants something done in time for the holidays. You know how it is."

Mrs. Delaphine's face took on certain gray lines and her eyes had a glistening flatness as she turned to him. "Miss Murdock surely takes time for lunch each day."

"Of course I do," Emily said. "I'd love to go to the Colony—I've never been near the place. But I haven't a thing to wear. Henry could go down to Bloomingdale's and get me a dress."

"I'll have nothing to do with it," Henry said, and returned to his striping job.

"Any little dress will do," Mrs. Delaphine said quickly, getting up. "I'll see you at noon tomorrow then, at my apartment. And don't forget your brushes, dear." She was gone.

"You dope." Henry turned to Emily. "She's working you, can't you see that?"

"Sure," Roscoe grunted. "She get you to paint for nothing."

"We'll send her a bill," Emily protested. "Just the same as if I didn't go to lunch. I think you're being awfully hard on her. She has money, Henry."

"Not much since Harmon left her. Of course it could be just a scheme to get you there on a certain day," he admitted grudgingly. "You are hard to pin down. And if you really want to go to the Colony, who are we to forbid it, eh, Roscoe?"

"Bad woman," Roscoe grumbled. "She don't mean no good to nobody. The doc was right to walk out."

Emily was biting the end of her brush and staring dreamily out the window.

"You'll never finish that thing by four o'clock if you don't get back to work," Henry prodded.

"Yes, I will." Emily squeezed out a blob of green and earnestly applied herself to the job of painting the word darling on a slot machine. One of the assorted Whitneys wished to present the slot machine to her husband on his birthday. "Anyway"—Emily turned round indignantly— "who's the boss here, Henry Bryce?"

"You are, of course," Henry bowed toward the splintered and paint-stained floor.

"Sometimes I wonder." Emily pursed her lips and went on with her work.

"You're the boss, but I have the brains," Henry added.

"That's what you get, Roscoe, when you take a person into your business and build him up and put your faith in him. I didn't have to give you a job, Henry Bryce."

Henry said, "No, you could have enjoyed a suit for damages instead."

"It wasn't my fault you broke your silly leg over that blackamoor."

"When I said you could store a few things in my apartment while I was in Alaska I thought you would leave an aisle from the bed to the bathroom."

"I did. There was just that one thing in between," Emily reminded him.

"And that one thing was black."

"He don't mean it, he's kidding, Miss Murdock," Roscoe put in, smiling from one to the other. "He really goes for you."

"Roscoe," Henry warned, "I thought you were my friend."

"He doesn't think any more of me than he does of that chest." Emily sighed.

"You're quite wrong. My paychecks come from you, darling." Henry slithered the brush around in the little pool of paint he kept on a piece of newspaper at his elbow, and as he did so he looked down into the street. There was his sister Cornelia, sleek and stately in a black coat and sable scarf. She was, as usual, crossing against the light.

Roscoe saw her too. "Here comes the troublemaker."

"Say who you mean," Emily complained. "I can't stop every few minutes and look out the window the way you two do. Is it Cornelia or Mrs. Cormorant?"

"Cornelia," Henry sighed. "Maybe she won't come up."

"She comes up." Roscoe nodded gloomily.

In a few minutes Cornelia pushed open the heavy metal door of the studio with a white-gloved hand. "Henry, you look ghastly. You're working too hard." She gave Emily a bitter glance and slipped the sable scarf from her shoulders.

"I have a cold," Henry told her.

"Then why don't you turn on the heat? It's as cold as a grave in here. Hello, Emily." She threw the greeting like a handful of wet mud, pulled out a cane-bottomed chair, and carefully sat down.

Cornelia, glistening in black and silver, made the studio seem suddenly very disorderly, completely inefficient, and supremely uncomfortable. Cornelia, who was such a picturesque failure herself, was acidly critical of other people's careers.

Roscoe put down his brush, blew his nose. "I go out for coffee," he suggested.

"Bring me half-a-dozen clams and a pastrami sandwich," Emily ordered.

"Pastrami for a lady who lunches at the Colony?" Henry asked. "Bring me one, too, Roscoe."

"Clams?" Roscoe asked at the door.

"Heaven forbid. You know how I feel about clams."

"Who's having lunch at the Colony?" Cornelia demanded.

"Emily. With your friend Mrs. Delaphine, tomorrow."

"No, really? How nice, Emily. Cleo didn't mention it to me." Henry could see that Cornelia was thinking this over. He didn't like to see Cornelia thinking about Emily at any time. Cornelia tolerated women if they were over eighty and very ugly, and her feelings about Emily were particularly resentful.

"What on earth are you doing to that ridiculous slot machine?" she demanded.

Emily told her that Mrs. Whitney wanted it by four o'clock.

"Which Mrs. Whitney?" Cornelia wanted to know.

"Mrs. Eli Whitney," Henry told her. "The inventor of gin."

"I don't think that's funny. Did James call me? He was to call me here at four o'clock." They said James had not called, and Cornelia went on, "Do you think he looks well? I don't, at all. He complains a great deal about his stomach."

"That's the ground glass you feed him," Henry suggested.

"Really, your humor has suffered from association with people who aren't quite bright. You know I'm fond of James, even if he will be sixty-one in January."

"We're all getting older," Emily said gently and probably without malice.

"I haven't begun to think of my age. I suppose I will when I pass forty."

"You mean you're making a return trip?" Henry inquired, hoping Cornelia would go. Early in the morning he could be polite to his sister, but by late afternoon, with a train of capricious private customers and eminent decorators behind him, he found Cornelia a heavy last straw.

"Have a lovely time at your luncheon," she said presently to Emily, and made her way around various obstacles to the door. "If James calls, tell him I've gone over to Cleo's."

Emily painted briskly until she heard the downstairs doors close, then, resting her elbow on the head of a short wooden priest in for repair, she demanded, "What's the matter with her eyes, Henry?"

"What do you mean?"

"She looks half awake, even when she's using a knife. You don't think she takes something, do you?"

"Of course not, Emily," he lied. He was sure Cornelia was taking veronal again.

"You know what?" Emily arranged two brushes on the priest's upper lip to look like a mustache. "I think she'd look better if she let her hair be gray."

Henry said she was afraid of growing old. "She's afraid of a lot of things, poor girl."

"Another thing, Henry. Has she ever said before that she was fond of Beansie? That sounded phony to me."

Henry shrugged. "All wives make those meaningless remarks sometimes. You'd better get back to work. It's quarter past four."

"Of course she ought to like him," Emily continued, vaguely dipping her brush and going back to the slot machine. "He's wonderful to her. How long is it since Cornelia pulled one of her stunts? It's about time she did something terrible again."

Henry groaned. "Let's not anticipate trouble. Anyway, she's been much better since she married James." He hoped she would stay better. There had been a day when any news of his sister was violent news—she had tried to jump off a plane on the way home from Bermuda, she had taken an overdose of sleeping pills in Mexico, she had pretended to lose a magnificent emerald on the Chief. In those days it had been Henry who picked up the pieces. Now it was James.

Emily had a look of heavy cerebration. "What makes a girl like Cornelia act that way? She's really beautiful, if you don't mind her expression, and she plays the piano nicely, and she has a brain."

"She didn't want to play the piano 'nicely,' as you put it. She wanted to play it brilliantly, but she hadn't the guts to stay with it eight or ten hours a day. Cornelia wants the universe wrapped in cellophane and delivered by a postman who never heard of C.O.D."

"James was a dope to marry her."

"I feel sorry for him," Henry agreed, "but the poor guy seems to enjoy it. And he's been good for Cornelia."

"She's been resting," Emily warned, pursing her lips and standing off to look at the slot machine. "She'll do something one of these days, and this time it's got to be something big, Henry. She really ought to kill herself, after all those trial runs. But you know she wouldn't want to kill herself, so maybe she'll knock off poor old Beansie instead. What a shock in Boston when they see his picture with the hole in his pale, aristocratic forehead."

"I shouldn't answer these absurd fantasies of yours, but may I point out the risk of electrocution? Do you think Cornelia would enjoy being executed?"

"She loves risky things," Emily insisted. "She likes to get as close to the edge as she can without falling in. The way I wait as long as I dare before I pay the gas bill. Just that narrow edge between will they shut off the gas or won't they."

Roscoe came back with the clams, sandwiches, and coffee, and put them on the worktable. "She is gone," he said with a broad smile. "*Bueno.*"

Emily gulped the clams in rapid succession, swallowed her sandwich, wiped her hands. "I've got to get into Bloomingdale's before five-thirty and buy a dress to wear tomorrow. Roscoe, next time you get pastrami, please ask them to put mustard on it, will you?"

"I wouldn't get a new dress just for Mrs. Delaphine," Henry protested.

"I'm afraid of her. Here I've got her on my own ground, but behind a knife and fork I know I'm going to be paralyzed. Henry, come with me and help pick out a dress?"

"No."

"If we were married you'd have to."

"I question that, and anyway, we're not."

"Why don't you marry me, Henry?" she asked, taking off the filthy smock.

"I'm too busy."

"Don't you want to marry me?"

Henry smiled. "Just because it's your studio you think you can ask me all these personal questions."

"But it would be so nice," Emily persisted. "You could go home early and pick up dinner at the delicatessen, and I could be finishing up odd jobs like this slot machine, and when I got to the apartment the bed would be made and the table would be set and candles lighted—"

"And Henry stewing on the back of the stove. No, dear. Let's leave things as they are. I like you, Emily. I want to go on liking you."

"Cornelia doesn't want you to marry me."

"No," Henry admitted, "but I'm not going to marry you just to irritate Cornelia."

Emily shrugged. "It's too bad. You're such a neat person, Henry. Would you marry me if I helped you paint your kitchen?"

"I don't think so, but you might try."

"I'll do it tomorrow night. After my big plunge into society."

Emily finally got herself into a hat and coat, and departed for Bloomingdale's, which was only a short walk down the avenue. Mrs. Whitney's chauffeur came for the slot machine, and Henry and Roscoe put the lids on the paint cans and closed the shop.

Henry walked slowly across Sixty-second Street. He was thinking, not too seriously, about Emily. He was very fond of Emily, but he didn't want to marry her. Not just now, at any rate. His first wife had thrown hot coffee in his face and cried all the time. He had no strong feelings of resentment toward her—there might, he suspected, be something in him that made women throw hot things and cry—but he hesitated to put his personality to the test for the second time. Emily had been married once too. Her husband, an engineer on the Long Island Railroad, proved allergic to the smell of paint, and as Emily would as soon die as give up painting, they had reluctantly separated.

Emily was attractive, and there was no doubt that she could have found another husband without much trouble. Link Simpson asked her to marry him at least twice a year. Wallace wanted her, and that was quite a compliment, since decorators rarely showed any interest in women except as check writers. But perversely, Emily would have Henry or nobody. They worked well together in the shop. It was a question, however, whether this peaceful arrangement would be marred by a closer association.

He walked down the two steps to the entrance to his building, glanced negligently at the pink stucco next door where Mrs. Delaphine worked out her luxuriously unhappy existence, and pulled out his keys.

"Hello there, Henry!" James Lord came across the street to speak to him. Henry asked him up for a drink although he didn't particularly want company at that moment.

"I'm waiting for Cornelia," James explained. "She's at Cleo's and I didn't want to go in and listen to a lot of hat and girdle talk, so I had a bit of a walk." He puffed slightly as he followed Henry up the narrow stairway and waited for him to open his door.

"Don't blame you," Henry said. "Mrs. Delaphine was in the studio today." He shed his coat and went into the kitchen. "She's bribing Emily to do some work for her."

"That so? I understood Cleo was rather short of money since the miserable Las Vegas swindle."

Henry said that for a woman who was short of money she had appeared amazingly sure of herself. "And rather cheerful, now that I think of it."

"Really?" James came and stood in the kitchen doorway regarding Henry with his worried hunting-dog frown. "I haven't seen her for more than a week. Perhaps she's come into something unexpected. Hope so. Cleo's a good sort."

"She's a spoiled, congenitally unhappy bitch and you know it." Henry dropped ice cubes into glasses.

"You're rough on the human race, Henry." James smiled, accepted the highball, and wandered over to the piano. He never played when Cornelia was present because she made fun of his precise, wooden notes. "Mind if I bang on it?"

"Go ahead." Henry lay back on his couch and watched him. It was a pity, he thought for the hundredth time, that a nice, orderly, kindly soul like James Lord should have got tangled up with Cornelia. It was probably some character Cornelia knew who had pulled off the swindle which was now weighing on James's mind. James and Cornelia had gone to California, by way of Arizona and Nevada. While they were gone about fifteen of James's friends had received urgent letters, apparently with his signature, suggesting investment in a silver mine near Las Vegas. The letters were mailed in Las Vegas, and money was to be wired to a Las Vegas bank. All in a great rush, of course. When James returned he was amazed and bewildered, since he had written no such letters. His time during the three months since his return had been mostly occupied with efforts to find the swindler. He had, Henry understood, given more than he could afford to some of his friends who were actually hard up, like old Christy.

"Any clues yet on Las Vegas?" Henry asked when James stopped playing.

"Not a thing. Bailey and Rousseau are working on it, they tell me, but so far no results. The police haven't come up with anything either."

"Who are Bailey and Rousseau?"

"Very good Boston firm, private detectives."

"This must be setting you back a good hunk of change," Henry suggested.

James said it would be worth anything it cost to find out who had robbed his friends. "Until the thing is run to ground I shan't rest."

"If I were you," Henry said easily, "I'd forget the whole thing. It was damned unfortunate, but you couldn't prevent it. And by this time all that money has been spent. You won't recover a cent even if you find out who did it. Damned clever fellow, whoever he was."

"I feel like a criminal," James confessed, taking a sip of the highball and looking bleak. "I dislike meeting my friends. When I see a bank I shudder. Even a telegraph office gives me a start."

Henry sympathized but he wasn't paying close attention. He looked around at his well-arranged and fairly spacious room. That was another thing about marrying Emily—she became attached to strange articles of furniture. She might even insist on keeping the Pullman section. A customer had ordered it decorated in *chinoiserie* four years ago, and then the customer had gone broke or died or moved away, and Emily was left with the thing which she promptly moved into her own apartment and used as a bed. She also had a couple of Florentine lanterns, public-library size. She wanted to work them off on a customer, but it wasn't everybody who would take two Florentine lanterns.

The phone rang. It was Emily, from Bloomingdale's. "Henry, they have the same dress in black and in green. Which shall I take?"

"I don't know. Which looks better?"

"I can't tell. I wish you'd come down and see."

"Emily," he groaned, "you surely must have picked out your own clothes before you knew me."

"But before I knew you it didn't matter, Henry."

"You don't look quite so fat in black."

"I'm not fat—I'm agreeably plump. But I do think the black is better," she added. "Somebody will be giving a funeral or a cocktail party and black is smarter at either one."

James was smiling. "She's quite a girl, Emily. I have the greatest affection for her, really."

"So have I," Henry admitted, "but I'd rather be responsible for a day-old chick."

The next morning Emily came in carrying her new dress in a box and her best hat in another box, and wearing a lot of jewelry and some hormone cream.

"Do you think I ought to go, Henry? I don't think I'll go."

"You know you wouldn't miss this damned lunch for all the turkey in Vermont."

"Oh, I would too. It doesn't mean a thing to me. Do you think my old hat is good enough?" She put it on in front of the cracked piece of mirror.

Roscoe, who was still working on the clock, gave the hat his critical scrutiny. "Beautiful, Miss Murdock."

"Thanks, Roscoe. I don't think you know, but anyway, thanks."

"You will not be eating pastrami sandwiches today, Miss Murdock. Maybe cold breast of chicken?"

"Guinea hen," Emily suggested, getting into her smock and blue jeans. "You know what I'm going to do this morning? Mrs. Wilbur Cormorant's bird cage."

"Why the rush? We've had it for three months."

"There will come a day when Mrs. Cormorant will drive right into the studio in her biggest car with her biggest mink coat and say, 'Miss Murdock, my bird cage, if you please.' "

Henry shrugged. "You must feel ambitious."

"I feel wonderful." Emily began moving chairs to get at the bird cage. Abruptly she ceased. "Henry, I don't think I'll go."

"Of course you'll go. Stop being a child."

The morning was feverish with Emily's hot and cold impulses. By eleven o'clock Henry and Roscoe were worn out.

She called her mother in Babylon to ask her advice. After a conversation consisting, on Emily's part, of "Yes, Mother," she hung up. "I'm sorry I even told her about it," she said irritably. " 'Emily, don't stare at people, be sure to use your napkin, don't gargle your soup.' Honestly, you'd think I was five years old."

"Almost," Henry said.

At half-past eleven she began to get ready, coming out of the washroom at the rear of the studio every few minutes to ask for opinions and encouragement. Finally she was dressed.

"Henry, go down and get me a cab," she said.

"A cab? It's only around the corner."

"I know, but I want to arrive in style."

"Very well. But stop shaking, she'll think you have the plague. What about your brushes and paint for the niches?"

She had forgotten about her materials, so Henry gathered them into a paper bag and escorted her downstairs. He got her into a cab, tipped the driver to make up for the short ride, and went over to Gottlieb's Delicatessen and Restaurant for his lunch.

At two o'clock Emily returned. She was smiling in a subdued way.

"How was it?" Henry asked.

"It was very nice," Emily said. "I did the niches and then Mrs. Delaphine said, 'I'm going to have a sandwich. Wouldn't you like one, too, Miss Murdock?' So Miss Murdock said, 'Of course,' and the maid brought in two lettuce sandwiches and two glasses of milk on a big silver tray, and we had lunch."

"What?"

"That's what."

"No Colony?" Roscoe regarded her with pity, then anger slowly rose in his face. "I will kill the woman!" he cried, picking up a hammer.

"No, Roscoe. We need you." Henry took the hammer. "Didn't she give any explanation?"

"None. She pretended to forget that she had ever asked me to go out to lunch."

"How long did you work?"

"About an hour, I think."

"Wait till she gets the bill. We'll take ourselves to lunch."

"If she ever pays the bill."

Emily, remarkably cheerful now that it was over, in fact rather amused at herself, got into her smock and set to work again on the bird cage.

"Bitch!" Roscoe spat into his private spittoon which was destined to be painted dove-gray and filled with philodendron for somebody's mistress on Park Avenue.

"Oh well," Emily sighed good-naturedly, "she can't help being a bitch. Henry, we're painting your kitchen tonight, aren't we? I'd like to celebrate in some way."

Henry agreed absently. He was putting green leaves on a commode, but he wasn't thinking about his work. He saw himself taking various forms of revenge on Mrs. Cleo Delaphine. He was delivering a truckload of moribund mackerel to the sidewalk in front of her house. He was calling upon her as a telephone repairman and disconnecting everything electrical in her house. He came as a plumber and made it impossible for her to enjoy the usual facilities of a human dwelling.

He noticed once that Roscoe had a black brooding look, more vengeful than anything he himself could put on, and he rather envied Roscoe his dark, lean face.

Emily and Henry had dinner at Gottlieb's Delicatessen, and at half-past eight they entered Henry's apartment and began to remove the dishes and pans from the kitchen.

"Henry, why don't you get rid of some of this stuff? What do you want with a Turkish coffeepot?"

"Suppose I meet a Turk someday—I couldn't give him Chemex."

Emily busily carried out plates and old-fashioned glasses and skillets, piling them on the floor in the other room. She paused beside two cans of paint. "What's this awful blue for?"

"I'm making it red, white, and blue."

"Henry, we decided on poison green."

"Maybe we did, but I decided on red, white, and blue. Put your smock on before you get paint all over yourself."

"Tyrant."

"I never order you to do anything you weren't going to do anyway."

"Would you like to order me to marry you?" she inquired, softening.

Henry, carrying the stepladder into the kitchen, didn't bother to answer that one. They went to work, painting steadily till eleven, when they paused for some blue cheese and crackers and coffee.

Emily said she had a headache. "I think I'll run over to the apartment and get my pills," she said. "And I can look for a better brush while I'm there. I don't like this one. It's too small."

"Why don't we quit for tonight, Emily? I'm bushed and you look awful."

"I'll be all right once I take a pill."

"I have some aspirin—wouldn't that do just as well?"

"No, I have these special things Dr. Quinlan gave me. I'll be right back." She snatched her coat and put it on over the paint-spattered smock. She could never be persuaded to have any regard for her clothes.

Henry smoked a couple of cigarettes, had a highball, and then Emily was back. She had, of course, forgotten the paintbrush but she explained that the pill was the important thing and she had remembered to take one.

At midnight Beardsley Satchel and his wife began to quarrel in the apartment over Henry's. Satchel, who divided his time between Wall Street and Charley's bar, was the problem of Henry's apartment building. Each building had one individual who was a drain on the other tenants, and Beardsley was their affliction. He had a mottled face like meat that isn't quite fresh, and small bloodshot eyes, and his collars were dirty where he ran a finger around inside. He complained a great deal about the lack of opportunity in the country. Martha, a stringy, sad-eyed brunette, loved him, cried at him, made excuses for him. Often she came in and told Henry her troubles, and he would give her a cup of coffee and try to find hope in the situation, although he couldn't really see any, short of Beardsley's sudden death. There was nothing so bad for some men as a good woman.

Beardsley went out presently, shouting all the way down the stairs to the street.

"That's one reason I don't want to marry you, Emily," Henry said. "I couldn't keep up a feud like that."

"You wouldn't have to, dear, I'd keep it up."

"I'm ready to drop in my tracks. Let's call it a night."

"No, we'll finish it. I want to see how it looks."

They went on working. Shortly after one they heard the crash of falling glass in the hall downstairs, and Henry said somebody had slammed the door too hard and broken the panes again.

At half-past one there was a knock at Henry's door. Satchel stood in the hall, a blood-soaked towel wound about his wrist. "Good evening, Bryce," he said politely while blood dripped from the towel to the floor. "I want to tell you I like your new topcoat."

"I'm glad," Henry said. "Could I get you something—an ambulance perhaps?"

"It's nothing." Beardsley waved a deprecating hand. "I've had a wonderful evening. Wonderful. Without liquor too. You can see I'm not drunk." He swayed dreamily.

Emily came up behind Henry and stared at the blood.

"How did you do it?" she asked.

"That?" He glanced idly at his wrist. "It's nothing. Henry, I saw your sister in Charley's. But that wasn't what I came to tell you, Henry. What was it? Oh—your topcoat. I like your topcoat."

"I think he's killed his wife," Emily whispered. "Get him away from here."

"Don't whisper," Satchel begged, "speak up. What do you suppose has happened to Martha? I don't hear a thing up there, do you?"

Henry gently led Mr. Satchel to the stairs and pushed him upward. "You go to bed now, Beardsley. You'll feel better in the morning—if you're not dead."

Emily was staring at the wainscoting in the hall. "He's murdered Martha," she whispered. "Henry, we'll be taken to jail. Look at the blood. Look at the floor."

"Don't be hysterical. Martha wasn't a very good neighbor anyway." Henry pushed her into the apartment and locked the door, then he picked up the phone, called the precinct station and reported Beardsley's accident. While he was doing this the buzzer sounded. "Let them in, Emily," he ordered.

Someone came up the stairs, stopped in the hall, knocked gently. Emily stood frozen. "I can't open the door, Henry. It's the F.B.I. They'll take you away."

Henry opened the door and Cornelia walked in, her eyes slightly glazed. "Your vestibule is full of broken glass," she said, flipping off her scarf.

"Beardsley did that," Henry told her. "He said he'd seen you in Charley's."

"Now don't scold, Henry. I've had three drinks the whole evening. Is that dissolute? Hello, Emily, I thought you'd be here. Working, of course."

The sarcasm was lost on Emily, who said brightly, "Yes, come and see."

Cornelia leaned in the kitchen doorway. "God, what colors. Your idea, Emily?"

"Mine," Henry said. "You're getting paint on your coat."

"Make me some coffee, Henry dear."

"How can I make coffee? I can't use the kitchen."

"You didn't paint the gas stove, did you?"

Henry glared at his sister. "It's almost two o'clock. I suppose you'd like me to take you home too."

"You're so sweet."

"James ought not to have let you out in the first place."

"He doesn't know I'm out. He's been in bed for hours."

"I suppose he'll think that odor you bring with you is new-mown hay."

Cornelia turned on him angrily. "I can't stay at home with him night after night. I'd go mad. What is there to talk about? How Jamesie caught a twenty-inch trout on his fourteenth birthday. James' deadly year at Cambridge. James' ghastly three years at Harvard. People are always talking about vice. Have you ever lived with virtue? James reeks of mean little virtues—he brushes his teeth three times a day—"

"Bad for the enamel," Emily put in gravely.

"He wouldn't cheat the government a nickel on his taxes. He sends birthday and Christmas cards to his five hundred and thirty relatives in and around Boston. He brings me flowers on Valentine's Day and candy every Saturday. He gets up early and makes coffee and serves me my breakfast in bed. I hate him!"

Henry shrugged. "He overlooks one little duty. He ought to beat you every Tuesday."

"Poor Beansie." Emily sighed.

Cornelia whirled. "That's what they all say—poor James, poor Mr. Lord. Never poor Cornelia!"

Henry was horrified to see that she was crying. He couldn't remember when he had seen Cornelia cry. It was very embarrassing. He didn't know what to do. "You need a good night's sleep," he said gently. "I'll take you home."

"I don't want to go home."

At that rather unfortunate moment the buzzer sounded and James came puffing up the stairs. "Greetings, everybody! I thought perhaps you'd be here, Cornelia." He had a pink, healthy glow even at that hour, and he brought with him a pleasant smell of fresh air and good cigar. "Cold out," he said. "May snow."

"Imagine that," Cornelia remarked bitterly. "What got you out of bed?"

James said he had felt like roaming around a bit, but it was perfectly obvious he had come looking for Cornelia.

"What's all the gore in your hall?" he asked.

Emily told him about Beardsley, and James made a clucking noise. "Poor Martha," he said.

"Isn't it a shame?" Cornelia agreed. "Some people have drunken husbands and others have drunken wives."

James didn't appear to hear this. "I stopped in Charley's. Link Simpson was there, seemed to be having a rather gloomy celebration all by himself."

"We should have asked him up," Emily said. "I thought he looked kind of sad today. Maybe I ought to phone him. James, come and see what we've done to Henry's kitchen. Careful of the paint. There— you've done it. On your lovely overcoat." She picked up a rag, soaked it with turpentine and rubbed at the spot.

"Emily," Cornelia said suddenly, "you haven't said a word about your lunch at the Colony. What did Cleo wear?"

"She wore a lettuce sandwich," Henry answered. "You couldn't possibly have put a monkey wrench in that luncheon, could you, Cornelia?"

"I? How absurd!" Cornelia smiled eagerly. "Tell me what happened, Emily. Did she find a way to get out of it, after you'd done the work?"

"I thought you and Cleo were friends," Henry reminded her.

"That's why I know her character so thoroughly. Cleo hates to see a dollar slip away, doesn't she, James?"

"You're tired, dear. Shall we clear out so your brother can get some sleep?" James stood up and buttoned his overcoat. "We'll see you across the street, Emily."

"Don't be tactless." Cornelia smiled. "She's staying all night."

"I can't." Emily sighed. "I didn't bring my pajamas." She wriggled into her coat and went off with Cornelia and James.

Chapter 2

"You know what I like about life?" Emily inquired before she had her hat off the next morning.

"No," Henry grunted, feeling very tired and not caring one way or the other. .

"You never know what's going to happen next." Emily set to work on the bird cage with enthusiasm and energy. It made Henry tired sometimes just to look at Emily. She never ran down. "Where's Roscoe?"

"His sister is probably having another baby at his expense." Henry arranged his paint and brush carefully, lighted a cigarette, delaying the moment of beginning to draw green lines on an ugly set of four white chairs destined to hold the posteriors of four female bridge players. He looked across the street. The Thinkers' lounge was still in darkness. Down on Lexington Avenue the slush was being spattered on nylon legs and the skittish wind off the East River was blowing Joey's papers around on the newsstand. Roscoe appeared, a familiar figure out of the mob, bought himself a paper from Joey, stepped off the curb after a study of the lights, and then started across the street while reading the paper. Henry watched him. Two taxis just missed him and Roscoe was not even aware of danger. In the middle of the street he stopped dead, staring at something which astonished his slow brain. Probably something about graft in City Hall—that always astonished Roscoe. Then he started to run, leaving a string of swearing drivers behind him. He ran up the stairs to the studio, slammed open the door.

"You see it?" he cried. "You see the news?"

Emily snatched the paper. "My God, Henry!" she said. "Look."

"What?" Henry grunted. Probably Robert Moses was tearing down St. Paul's to put up a bridge to Jersey.

" 'The body of Mrs. Harmon Delaphine was found early this morning by her maid. Police say she was killed by a shot from a revolver at close range.' " Emily looked up. "Henry, did you hear what I just read you?"

"I heard it. I'm digesting it." Henry took the paper to read the account for himself. There were few details. Apparently the story had broken too late for the *Tribune*, which he always bought. "No gun found on the scene," he remarked.

"You think she shot herself?" Roscoe inquired.

"Sure, and walked over to Park Avenue, dropped the gun through the subway grating, returned to her apartment, and lay down."

"Don't tease Roscoe," Emily said. "He doesn't know about murders."

Roscoe was indignant; he knew all about murders. "I read the *Mirror* every night."

"You didn't kill her, Roscoe," Henry asked, "because she wouldn't take Miss Murdock to lunch?"

Roscoe had a disappointed look. "I wish I would of. I'm sorry, Miss Murdock, but I didn't kill your friend."

"That's all right, Roscoe—Henry, you mean if they don't find a gun at a place where a person has been shot then the person was murdered?"

"Yes, dear."

"Oh." Emily shuddered slightly, dipped her brush, and began to put a Chinese design on the bottom of the cage. "Anyway, we didn't do it. I was with you and you were with me all evening."

Henry pointed out that they didn't know when she was killed.

"Well, if she was shot before two, we're in the clear."

"You're not worried, are you? I see no reason why the thing should involve us at all. She's a customer, not a friend." Henry picked up the phone.

"Calling Homicide?" Emily asked.

"This isn't a movie, Emily. Stop acting. I'm going to tell James and Cornelia. They probably haven't heard."

James answered the phone—Cornelia was still in bed. "I say," he exclaimed. "I say, what a dreadful piece of news." James would have given the same response to an inferior lettuce salad or a world revolution. "Murdered, did you say? Sounds a bit farfetched, don't you think?"

"Very," Henry agreed. "But there have been a good many robberies the past few months and maybe Cleo put up a fight. I rather think she would, don't you? Come on down and we'll hash it over. Perhaps the next edition of the papers will carry the solution. It may be a very simple case, robbery or a mad janitor or something like that." Henry hung up. "Poor old James is in a dither. A well-bred dither, of course."

Emily stopped painting, letting the brush drip on the floor. "He thinks Cornelia did it."

"Such an idea would never enter his head. He worships Cornelia."

"Anyway, she did it. Didn't I tell you yesterday she had to do something big this time?"

Roscoe looked frightened. "You believe this, Miss Murdock?"

"Don't listen to her, Roscoe," Henry advised. "When are you going to finish that damned clock? You've been at it for two solid days."

Roscoe apologized, and then Henry remembered that there had been an interruption to deliver a screen to Brooklyn Heights and another to paint a pair of beds black. Roscoe was too polite to argue. He was so polite and so gentle it was impossible to imagine his pointing a gun at anyone, and yet, for Emily, he would have done anything in the world. Well, if Roscoe had shot Mrs. Delaphine it would come out before long, because he was too simple to conceal anything. If he took salts, he had to tell somebody, usually Emily.

Link Simpson came tearing into the studio, smiling. "Isn't it delightful? Did you ever hear of anything more appropriate? Rich dowager reneges on luncheon date with poor decorator and next morning is found dead, shot, murdered, done in! I love it. I positively love it." He dropped his long, limp frame into a Louis armchair and fanned himself with the newspaper. "Poor, poor Cleo. My heart bleeds. Ha!"

"Don't be so happy when you talk to the police," Emily warned. "I wish they'd come. The suspense is awful."

"What makes you think they'll come to see us?" Henry demanded.

"You mean they won't? But they've got to. If they don't, I'll call up and complain."

"I hope the check she gave me yesterday goes through," Link

remarked. "Do you think they might hold it up, Henry?"

Henry didn't think so. "You were smart to get a check. We didn't."

Link looked suddenly less happy. "I wonder what time she was killed. I delivered those damned girandoles to her house around eight last night."

"Link!" Emily turned frightened eyes on him. "You were in her house last night? You were alone with her?"

"Absolutely. I knew that old story about needing the stuff for a party was a gag. She wasn't having a party."

"She was, but she didn't know it," Henry said.

"How did she look when you were there?" Emily demanded. "Was she nervous?"

"Not in the least. She had an expression of complete self-satisfaction. Something like a stuffed salmon mounted on a board."

Emily said maybe they would find Link was the last person to see her alive—except the murderer, of course. "Link," she added, "would you mind going back to the washroom and getting me the box of tissues? My nose is running."

Link said certainly, and went to the back of the studio, and while he was there James came in.

"I went out at once and purchased a paper," James said, looking quite haggard and breathing hard. "I had to see for myself. Still I can scarcely believe that Cleo—What do you think of it, Bryce?"

"Progress is inevitable." Henry fastened a critical eye on James's shirt front. "Do you realize, Lord, that your third and fourth buttons are undone?"

"My haste," James said, flushing. "I'm unnerved."

"Sit down," Henry offered. "Be unnerved in comfort."

"Thank you." James sat, took out his reading glasses and reread the item in the paper.

Link handed Emily the Kleenex and said he would like to stay and hash things over but he didn't dare leave the shop too long with Chauncey in charge. Chauncey was inclined to give things away when he was drinking, and he was always drinking.

"Why don't you fire him?" Henry asked.

"Where would the old buzzard find another job? Anyway, who am I to condemn the excessive consumption of alcohol?" He inspected his face in Emily's cracked bit of mirror.

"You really hung one on last night, didn't you?" James remarked.

"If I'd known the old bitch was going to be dead in a matter of hours I shouldn't have wasted all that rage on her."

"What rage?" Emily wanted to know.

"She got under my skin. I couldn't help mentioning the dirty trick she played on Emily, and she said some cutting things. Then I said some cutting things. By the time I got out of her lousy house I was ready to bite bricks. I got to thinking how I spend my life dealing with useless and vicious women like that, selling and reselling the same old junk just to keep them amused."

"It keeps you in food and liquor, too, Link," Henry reminded him.

"I know. But I wasn't being logical last night. I was mad. I took a hell of a long walk over to the river, and then I came back and got drunk in Charley's."

Emily gave him an anxious frown. "You mean you were alone for a long time last night?"

"Emily is playing Mr. District Attorney this week, Link. Don't mind her," Henry advised. "Half an hour ago she was sure Cornelia shot Mrs. Delaphine. Now she's giving you that look."

James perked up an ear. "Cornelia? Emily, I'm shocked at you."

"Oh, it was just a passing idea," Emily said lightly.

Link grinned. "Let me know what goes on from time to time, will you?" he said, and left.

James turned to Henry. "What shall we do about Harmon?"

"Harmon?"

"Yes. Is a note of sympathy in order, or is it in poor taste when—when—"

"When an ex-wife is shot? I'd let Harmon alone if I were you. The police will undoubtedly give him plenty of attention."

"I'd forgotten all about Dr. Delaphine," Emily said thoughtfully. "Do you think an analyst feels different than other people—I mean normal abnormal people like us—when a wife or something gets murdered? He couldn't be upset, could he? If you're upset you're maladjusted."

"James," Henry said, "would you mind getting up? I need that chair."

James wandered about the studio, picking things up, reading labels, tapping the surfaces and saying "Hmm." His secret opinion of decorating, Henry felt sure, was low. James believed that if a piece of furniture was good it was sacrilege to paint it, and if it wasn't good one shouldn't have it around. He and Cornelia had had a historic struggle over an upright Chickering inherited from James's aunt in Northampton. Cornelia had finally managed to give it to a school, but James still mentioned it wistfully.

"I didn't tell Cornelia about Cleo," he said. "She was asleep when I left and I didn't like to wake her. Well, I'll be going along. I'll call you if I hear anything."

It turned out to be a very social morning. In fact Henry accomplished almost nothing between conversations and trips down to the avenue for new editions of the papers and containers of coffee from the drugstore.

Hilda Leghorn came over from her beauty parlor across the street and wanted all the details in three minutes while somebody's hair was taking a bleach.

"Isn't it exciting?" Emily asked, when she had told Hilda all they knew.

Hilda shrugged, turned up her insolent nose. "I don't know," she said. "Too bad I did her hair this week. They'll do it over again. They always do." She cast her eye around the studio. "God, the junk you people have in here. Emily, why don't you open a high-class antique shop, with genuine antiques?"

Emily said apologetically that her business was making new antiques.

"But why don't you have a very lovely shop on Fifty-seventh Street? Like Alice Sydnam's?"

"Emily couldn't be that clean," Henry explained good-naturedly.

When Hilda had gone Emily said, "I hate people who say, 'Why don't you?' "

"Then why do you see so much of Hilda?"

"She's my best friend, Henry."

Just before lunchtime Harmon Delaphine arrived. He hadn't been in the studio for more than a year.

"Hello," he said, slightly self-conscious. "Thought I'd drop by."

"Glad to see you." Henry pulled out a chair for him. "Rather a shock to you, the news this morning."

"Yes. Yes, I was shocked. I went to the house at once. Her maid called me." Harmon didn't sit down. He was a short, solidly built man with a black mustache to strengthen his upper lip and a Phi-Bet key on his watch chain to increase his importance. Ladies went to Harmon instead of the Gypsy Tea Kettle. Analysis was fashionable, and after a certain age your past was more interesting than your future. His fees were enormous, and he had more patients than he could take care of. Henry felt uncomfortable with Delaphine. Perhaps it wasn't so at all, but Henry had the feeling that those sardonic brown eyes were reading psychopathic meanings into everything he did or said. To Harmon, nothing was what it appeared. An egg wasn't an article of breakfast nourishment, but evidence of sex life in poultry.

"It's too bad she was murdered," Emily said judiciously, "but I didn't like her. Did you?"

"Bright question number seventy-six," Henry grunted, rescuing Delaphine, who looked a little embarrassed.

"I don't see anything wrong with it," Emily persisted. "Harmon was married to her. He ought to know whether he liked her or not."

"He happens to have divorced her," Henry pointed out.

"Divorce doesn't mean dislike," Delaphine put in deliberately. "Not necessarily. Just an inability to live happily together."

"It was her fault, wasn't it?" Emily demanded.

Henry explained that Emily was feeling a little bitter toward the late Mrs. Delaphine because of a luncheon engagement. Harmon smiled bitterly, remarked that the action was characteristic. "Cleo always regretted a generous impulse. She didn't have many of them."

"I imagine you're glad she's dead, aren't you?" Emily inquired. "It must be a relief to you, Harmon."

Henry sighed, but he didn't say anything. Let Delaphine take care of himself.

"Cleo never matured emotionally," Harmon answered deftly. "As a child she was starved for affection. She never could believe that anyone was really fond of her for herself. She was sure I married her for her money."

"Did you?" Emily smiled brightly, wiping a paintbrush.

"I did not." Harmon was emphatic. "Have you heard that Cleo was rather hard pressed financially?"

"Yes," Henry answered. "Lord says she was had for a considerable chunk of cash on that Las Vegas deal."

Harmon had a thoughtful look now as he stood picking at a piece of loose veneer on a table. "She told me that, but I didn't know whether it was true or not."

"I suppose she wanted you to give her more alimony," Emily remarked. "Now you won't have to worry about her." Emily paused a moment, tapping her teeth with the handle of a paintbrush. "I think she committed suicide," she announced. "Mrs. Delaphine had an awful lot of fillings. Sometimes when I look at my back teeth practically honeycombed with dental constructions I feel like ending it all. When your teeth are gone, what have you, really?"

Henry said he had been wondering why the murderer hadn't tried to make it look like suicide. It seemed like a good setup. Harmon said he probably wasn't prepared, didn't intend to shoot her.

"Of course," Emily agreed. "Do you carry around sample suicide notes and guns and stuff?"

"He shot her with a gun," Henry argued. "Why not leave that gun in her hand?"

"He was too scared to think. If I did a thing like that I'd be so rattled I wouldn't know which end was up."

Henry said she didn't anyway. Delaphine appeared to enjoy this exchange, although his movements as he wandered about the studio were somewhat nervous. He kept looking at his watch, and finally left, quite abruptly.

"I wonder what he wanted?" Emily asked, watching him cross Lexington Avenue briskly, his well-tailored overcoat flapping in the sharp wind.

"You were certainly rough with him," Henry said reproachfully. "First time I ever saw Harmon at a loss."

"I think he's afraid. Naturally they're going to say he shot her."

"Why naturally?"

"A husband is the most logical person to shoot a woman, isn't he?" She paused. "But I still want to marry you, Henry."

At twelve o'clock Emily got a call from an old admirer, Clarence Mould. Henry listened but he couldn't make anything of it. Emily kept saying, "But I'd be afraid to do that, Clarence dear. She might just happen to remember he's here."

"What does he want?" Henry interrupted.

"He wants to borrow Daniel Webster. He had one, but it got broken and the play is opening tonight and he's in a spot."

"Mrs. Giddings' Webster? After three years it should be safe. What does Mould want to pay?"

Emily asked him. "He says anything we want to charge. He's desperate. But, Henry, I don't think it's right. The bust belongs to Mrs. Giddings, and if she found out she might be a little irritated."

Henry shrugged. "Use your own judgment."

Emily turned back to the phone. "It's all right, Clarence. You can have it. But it's only a loan, you understand? Because she might just happen to remember. Although they don't usually. We had an armchair here for five years, and finally I painted it up and gave it to a girl for a wedding present, and the woman who brought it here has never come back for it. They don't know what they have, really, Clarence. Isn't money wonderful? When do you want Daniel? All right, dear." She hung up. "He wants it by six, Henry. The Belasco is on Forty-fourth Street. You could take it around on your way home."

"I always go from Sixty-first Street to Sixty-second by way of Forty-fourth Street," Henry agreed. "You'll have to do some work on that bust—I remember something about a missing ear. You've still got to finish the bird cage, and what about the screen for Di Nobili?"

"I'll get all that done in nothing flat," Emily said airily. Emily was a perpetual optimist.

Link Simpson came up again. "I thought maybe we ought to take Emily out to lunch, Henry, in view of yesterday's fiasco."

"Aren't you nice," Emily smiled. "We're turning criminal, Link. We're renting out Mrs. Giddings' bust to the Belasco Theatre."

"Nice substantial property. What are you doing with the rest of Mrs. Giddings?"

Henry explained, adding that after three years they thought it was safe. Link had a doubtful look, which puzzled Henry. Link was generally in favor of a liberal interpretation of the Ten Commandments. "If you think it's worth the risk," he said.

"Suppose she does find out?" Emily countered. "She ought to be flattered to have her bust at an opening."

"Was Harmon Delaphine in to see you?" Link asked.

Henry said he had been, and Link told them that Delaphine had stopped in to talk to him too. "I don't know what he was trying to find out," Link went on. "I didn't mention my little session with his wife. I didn't think it was any of his business."

"You know what I think?" Emily demanded. "He knows something and he wants to find out if anybody else knows it."

"Undoubtedly," Henry grunted. "Did someone mention lunch?"

"Let's go to Keen's so we can take a taxi," Emily proposed. "Their food is very substantial too."

They agreed to take her anywhere she wanted to go, although neither Link nor Henry could find a spot on Emily which required the addition of substance.

It was half-past two when they got back, and Roscoe was anxious. "People come, people call up," he said. "I can do nothing. Besides business, comes the sister, Mrs. Lord."

"What did she want?" Henry asked.

"Who knows? She pit-pats up and down like big cat, looking here, poking there. She ask me six times where you go eat. How do I know where you go eat? Restaurant, I say. With taxi. Style."

In a few minutes Cornelia telephoned. "A thing like this, when it happens to a dear friend," Cornelia said, "is really dreadful."

"If it happened to a dear friend it would be."

"Henry, we may have had our little spats, but Cleo and I were very close. I feel terrible, I really do. I'm sure it was a thief, although they say there's nothing missing. How do they know whether anything's missing?"

Henry pointed out that Cleo's handbag, containing more than fifty dollars, was on a table in the room. There were rings and a bracelet left on the body. That had come out in the afternoon papers, along with a picture of Harmon Delaphine and the amount of the alimony he was paying Cleo.

"Is Cornelia enjoying it?" Emily asked, when he hung up.

"Undoubtedly."

It was half-past five when Emily finished the screen for Di Nobili and said she was ready for Daniel Webster. Henry went to the back of the shop to look for the bust and found it where it had rested for the last three years on the shelf of a Queen Anne bookcase which had also long been promised to somebody. He wiped off the dust.

"Nose is pretty badly chipped, Emily," he said. "One ear is gone."

Emily remembered that the ear had been severed by the man who came to plaster the ceiling when it fell down. "I thought we saved the ear. Roscoe, look in that box with the doorknobs and stuff."

Roscoe found it, and Emily set to work.

Henry returned to the monotonous job of striping the bridge chairs.

There was a rattle and a metallic thud. Emily screamed and Roscoe let out a whistle.

"Now what?" Henry demanded.

"Look!" she squeaked, pointing at the floor.

"It's a gun," Henry said stupidly. "Where did it come from?"

"Out of Daniel Webster."

"Now look here, Emily."

"It did. It was inside him."

"That's the truth, Mr. Bryce," Roscoe put in.

"What shall we do with it?" Emily demanded.

"Call the police and give it to them."

"You know what happens when you tell the police you've found a gun, don't you? They take you to jail. A woman on my mother's street in Babylon spent the night in jail because she found a gun on a bus and did the right thing and called the police."

"That's right," Roscoe said. "I heard that too."

Henry looked thoughtful. "I still think it's the only thing to do." He bent down.

"Don't touch it!"

"Are we going to leave it here and build a stile over it? We've got to touch it."

"It may have fingerprints on it."

"Sure." Roscoe put his oar in again.

"Suppose it has? Everything has fingerprints on it, even a box of cornflakes. It's probably been in that bust for the last fifty years." He said this to convince Emily, but he didn't believe it very firmly himself.

"You know who put it there, Henry? The person who shot Mrs. Delaphine."

"Oh, nonsense. That gun is down the sewer somewhere." Henry picked it up carefully, smelled it.

"It smells like powder, doesn't it?"

"Not to me. You smell it." He held it under her nose.

"More like a whiff of Two-in-One oil. Henry, stay away from that phone. You're not going to call the police."

"But you've got to report a thing like this."

"Who says you do?"

"Sure, who says so?" Roscoe demanded.

"Roscoe, will you kindly shut up and let me think?" Henry pleaded.

"Suppose one of our friends was using Daniel as a hiding place," Emily suggested, "do you want to betray his trust in us?"

Henry was about to remark that it was a strange sort of friend who would plant a gun in their workshop, but he knew it was useless to argue with Emily. He sat down and lighted a cigarette. "You take care of it, boss," he said.

The light that often crossed her face in her more inspired moments of unreason now made its appearance. Emily took some picture wire from a drawer, bored two holes in Webster's neck, and wired the gun inside the bust. "This time it's going to stay put," she said.

"Of course no one will be curious about that wire."

"I'm going to plaster over it and they'll think he had a mole." Emily could do anything with plaster and paint.

"What you're doing is illegal," Henry observed, "but perhaps it's the simplest way to dispose of a gun."

Emily had almost completed the repairs to the nose and ear when Link came in. "I have a date in the Village," he said. "Could I deliver Daniel Webster for you, on my way down?"

"He isn't finished," Emily told him nervously, and turned the bust so that Link couldn't see the lump on the neck.

"I'm the delivery boy," Henry put in. "Who's the girl this time, Link?"

"Just Doris." Link gave Emily a wistful look, said good night.

"Do you think we should have told him about the gun?" Emily asked, going to the window. "There, he's found a cab already. Link is good about things like that. Some people have to stand in the gutter half an hour before a cab will stop for them."

"I resent being called 'some people.' Link would be glad to hail cabs for you if you'd let him."

Emily frowned, rubbed her forehead with a grimy hand. "Do you think he's really going to see Doris, or has he found a new girl?"

Henry grunted. "You can't talk and work, too, so please stop talking. Roscoe and I want to go home."

The phone rang. It was Clarence Mould, nervous about delivery of the bust. Emily reassured him, turned to Henry. "Clarence can get us tickets for tonight if we want to go. Do we?"

"I'll go if you'll be on time," Henry agreed. "What's the play?"

"Oh, something about people."

James called a little later, looking for Cornelia. He was always look-ing for Cornelia, poor man. Henry tried to be comforting. "She's prob-ably shopping," he said.

"I hope you're right. But you know how excitable Cornelia is—and with all this business going on. The police paid us a call, by the way."

"Already?" Henry was surprised.

"They're working through Cleo's friends, it seems. Very courteous young man—a Mr. Burgreen. But all the same I can't say I enjoyed it."

"Have they found the gun?"

James didn't think so. "I haven't even heard what type of gun it was."

"Let me talk to Beansie." Emily took the phone. "Don't you worry about Cornelia," she told him. "She loves excitement, she's enjoying the whole thing. Could you have dinner with us, in case she isn't back by that time?"

"Emily," Henry groaned, "what about the theater?"

"Oh, I'm sorry, Beansie. You can't have dinner with us because we're not having any. We're going to the opening of a play—Clarence Mould is giving us tickets. Because we're letting him borrow Daniel Webster for a few days—you remember the bust Mrs. Giddings left here a few short years ago?"

Henry could hear James chuckle, and Emily, with a final word of comfort, hung up.

"One more interruption and we won't be able to deliver the damned plaster before curtain time," Henry grumbled.

Emily, unruffled, went back to work on the great man's nose. "Roscoe, did you wrap the bird cage for Mrs. Cormorant? I told you you'd have to deliver that on your way home."

"I got it all ready, Miss Murdock. In the back."

Henry and Roscoe sat waiting for her to finish. Henry stared across the avenue at the orderly comfort of the Thinkers' Club. No weapons, he felt sure, would ever disturb that rosy calm. A short bald man came to the window, stood looking out at the thinly falling snow. Presently a bellhop approached him with a glass of water on a tray. The little man took a tiny box from his pocket, popped something into his mouth, and swallowed the water. A bicarbonate addict, probably.

"It's finished," Emily said. "Wrap it up, Roscoe."

Roscoe carried Webster tenderly to the wrapping table at the rear of the studio.

"Use plenty of paper," Henry advised, "it's snowing." He took off his apron and got into his coat and tie. "Now, Emily, let's plan this so we can see the whole play. Will you promise to be ready at eight?"

"Henry, it's almost seven now. How can I eat something, get up to the apartment, and dress by eight?"

"I don't know, but that's when I'm coming for you, and I won't wait."

After adding footnotes to this ultimatum Henry put on his overcoat, took the heavily wrapped Mr. Webster under his arm, and went down to the street. It was snowing fast now, big wet flakes, and everybody in the city wanted a cab. He stood at the curb, waving and whistling, while the snow slid down his neck, melted on his nose, ran down his chin, blew into his ears.

"Hello, errand boy." It was Cornelia. "Lovely weather to be delivering packages."

"Your husband is looking for you," he grunted.

"What's in it?" She tapped the package with a gloved hand.

"Daniel Webster and a fried egg. Run along, will you? I'm busy."

Cornelia shrugged. "Going downtown? You might give me a lift to Fifty-fifth Street. Here's a cab."

He knew that giving Cornelia a lift would delay him, but it was a mean night. He let her get in.

"James says the police paid you a visit," he remarked.

"Me?" The question was sharp.

"Both of you, dear. He said they were going through the list of Cleo's friends. By the way, you once had a gun, didn't you, Cornelia?"

She stared coldly. "You do make the nicest small talk, Henry." They stopped in front of her apartment building and Cornelia got out, slammed the door without thanking him.

Henry had the bad habit of helping the driver drive. He sat forward as they tore down Park Avenue, the tires sucking and hissing on the wet pavement, rounded the Grand Central Concourse, and threaded their way perilously into Forty-fifth Street. Later, when he tried to remember that ride, he couldn't say that he had noticed anyone trying to follow his cab. In fact, he doubted if anyone could be certain of such a thing during a ride of some twenty blocks through suppertime traffic. They went west on Forty-fifth, came back on Forty-fourth, and stopped in front of the Belasco Theatre. It was snowing so fast now that you could scarcely see across the street. Nobody was out who didn't have to be, and Henry, as he paid the driver, wondered whether it was worthwhile to come back here again for the play.

The cab pulled away, he turned toward the stage entrance, and in an instant he was relieved of the burden of thinking.

He couldn't have been hit very hard, Henry decided, because after somebody stepped over him and said, "Wouldn't you think he'd fall down where he does his drinking?" he sat up and looked at his watch. It was twenty minutes of eight. A cop strolling by on his way to a cup of coffee said tenderly, "Anything wrong?"

Henry got up, brushed the snow from his clothes, and said he guessed he had slipped. The cop went on. No crowd gathered because everybody was so intent on getting where he was going in the storm. The package was gone. There was no doubt in Henry's mind that whoever had hit him had taken the bust.

The curtain was due to go up in an hour. Mould would be furious. Perhaps he could find another bust of Daniel Webster for him, Henry thought, recalling an auction room on Forty-fifth Street near Fifth Avenue. He waved in vain for another cab—several went by, but they were occupied. He started to walk, feeling a little shaky, and finally reached the place. It was closed, locked up tight till Monday morning. He stood there wondering what to do, feeling the cold moisture creep through the soles of his shoes. Probably get pneumonia, thanks to Clarence Mould.

No use calling Emily, it would just upset her. Then he remembered that Link had a couple of busts in his shop, probably not Webster, but in a pinch he thought Clarence would be glad to get any great man. He made his way to Sixth Avenue and a telephone, got Link at his girl's apartment, and told him he had lost the bust.

"How could you lose a five-pound package on your way downtown?" Link demanded.

"Somebody hit me on the head and took it."

"Oh, come on," Link scoffed. "Is this your idea of a joke?"

"It's no joke. Mould's show goes on at eight-forty and he's going to skin us alive if he doesn't have some kind of statue. What have you got in the shop?"

Link said he had Sherman and Erasmus, and Henry said he thought Sherman would be fine.

"You have a key to my place," Link reminded him. "Go in and help yourself."

"Emily has it. And I don't want to tell her what happened to me. You know how Emily is."

"All right," Link agreed, "I'll meet you at the shop as soon as I can get there."

Henry went down into the clammy stalactite regions of the Independent Subway and took a Queens train to Lexington Avenue. He was shivering, and his attention was divided between the pressing business of getting back to the Belasco with some kind of substitute for Daniel and the growing certainty that he was coming down with a horrible cold. Link had been lucky, as usual, and found a cab. He was waiting when Henry got there.

"Now tell me what really happened," Link demanded, carefully dusting off Sherman's beard and wrapping him in tissue paper.

"I was walking toward the stage door of the theater with Webster under my arm when somebody came along behind me and cracked me on the head. When I came to, the bust was gone."

"You mean somebody stole that ancient piece of rather poor plaster?"

"They were after the gun, Link."

Link stared. "What? You didn't happen to mention a gun."

"Emily found it when she was repairing the bust. It was hidden in his neck. Scared the wits out of her."

Link was rarely inarticulate, but for a full three seconds he just looked at Henry. "What did you do with it?"

"Against my advice, judgment, and dire warnings, Emily insisted on wiring the gun inside the bust. She tells me it isn't safe to report a gun to the police. But let's be on our way, Link. You'll come back with me, won't you? I wouldn't like to go through that again—not that I think there's any real danger—but I just have a certain distaste for the stage door of the Belasco."

Link said he would have a fine time explaining his absence to Doris, but he would come along. They caught a taxi and on the way back to

Forty-fourth Street he said with growing excitement, "Henry, that gun must be red-hot. It isn't just an old gun that somebody hid there a long time ago."

"That's what I've been thinking," Henry agreed.

"What caliber was it?"

Henry said he didn't know, he wasn't familiar with guns. "It was small. You could carry it around handily. I suppose the person who placed it inside the bust didn't expect Daniel to be moved."

"Who would?" Link inquired. "Emily's had that thing for three years, at least. The chances were very good that it would be there another three, unless Mrs. Giddings happened to remember it." He looked at Henry. "Do you think that gun killed Mrs. Delaphine?"

Henry grinned. "Do you?"

Link shrugged. "You should have turned it in, Emily notwithstanding. You could get into a lot of trouble."

They had arrived at the theater and Link took a look at the snow-covered sidewalk while Henry paid the driver. "The mark of your re-clining form is still here," he said, grinning. "I'm beginning to believe you."

They found Clarence Mould at the center of a frenzied knot of people, wearing an armful of paisley shawls. He accepted the bust of Sherman absently, and Henry and Link hurried out before he had time to unwrap it.

Henry thanked Link and then, feeling like a human shuttle, made his way once more uptown to Sixty-second Street and rang Emily's bell.

"Henry Bryce! Where have you been?" Emily demanded, slamming the door after him and then beginning to race around the room after the things she had forgotten to put into her bag. "Do you realize what time it is?"

Henry sat down. He felt a little sick. "I guess I'm late," he admitted humbly.

Emily looked at him, yanking on her slightly worn sable-dyed musk-rat. "You look awfully funny, Henry. What did you have for dinner?"

"Nothing."

She stopped short. "You're kidding."

"Nothing, I said."

"But you always eat dinner. Do you need vitamins?"

"I've been very busy since I saw you. Had the devil of a time getting a cab and then we were tied up in traffic, and then they wouldn't let me into the theater without a presidential pass. I'm beat." He stretched his legs and lay back on his spine, as well as he could in Emily's Victorian walnut side chair.

"I don't know whether to believe you or not. If this is just an act to disguise the fact that you're about an hour late, I'll take it out in blood. Meanwhile, maybe I'd better fry you an egg."

"I'd rather have a drink. I'm getting pneumonia."

"You can't have a drink. All I've got is the Hennessy that Mrs. Cormorant gave you when you did that ghastly pink-and-blue cherub."

Henry pointed out that the brandy was rightfully his, but he didn't get any of it. Emily said it was for an emergency, and this was not.

"I hope greater ones don't arise," he muttered.

"What was that?" She didn't wait for an answer but went into the kitchenette and scrambled two eggs, put them between slices of bread, dropped the whole into a paper bag, and handed it to Henry. "You can eat on the way. Come on."

Henry was too weak to fight. He followed Emily down the stairs and into a taxi. Some of the egg slid out on his lap. He tried a bite of the stuff. "It would have been thoughtful of you to cut the bread in two," he complained.

"That's the way with men. Give them a sandwich and they want a linen tablecloth. Here we are. It must be awfully late; there's nobody waiting."

Henry got out, carefully leaving the bag behind him.

"Heh, sir," the driver called, "you forgot your package."

Henry took it and they went inside where the first act was well under way. Their seats were in the center of the twelfth row and angry toes and knees drew back to let them pass while Emily made little clucking noises of apology. Henry didn't feel the bottom of the bag going, but just before he sat down there was a sudden deposit of egg and bread at the feet of a gentleman resembling the late C. Aubrey Smith. Some doubt as to its origin might have prevailed if Emily hadn't whispered shrilly, "What happened?"

There were shushes and groans. Henry helped her take off her coat. She dug in her bag, came up with some Charms, popped one into her mouth, and crunched enjoyably while fastening her eyes on the stage. Henry sighed, settled back. It was a pleasant setting, at least—a living room in a Southern house, with an air of wealth, summer, and relaxation. Sherman's plaster image stood on a walnut pedestal near an open window.

Emily sat forward. "Henry!" she cried, "it's the wrong bust!"

"Shh," he begged.

"But look, it isn't Webster. It's a man with a beard!"

"I know," he whispered. "I'll tell you later."

"Tell me now."

"Emily, please. People want to hear the play."

She was quiet, miraculously, till the intermission. They went out the side where the sandwich was not and, gaining the fresh air and the comparative privacy of a doorway, Henry told her what had happened. If he had felt stronger he would have invented something so that Emily wouldn't become alarmed. However, she took it very well.

"There isn't much of a bump," she said, feeling his skull. "Why do you think they wanted the bust, Henry?"

"They wanted the gun."

"Oh. So it wasn't just an old gun that had been sticking up Daniel Webster's neck for the last twenty years?"

Henry admitted that it didn't look that way.

"I told you it was the gun that killed Mrs. Delaphine. Now maybe you'll give more weight to my words." The warning buzzer sounded and Emily dropped her cigarette into a sand jar. "I think he was silly. Where would a gun be better hidden than inside a stage property?"

"Perhaps he was afraid the bust might be broken and the gun discovered," Henry suggested, following her back to their seats. "That's Link's theory, anyway."

"You told Link?"

"I had to. How would it sound otherwise to say someone had slugged me and stolen a plaster bust? Very improbable. Very alcoholic."

Emily took out some more Charms and munched, reading her program. "Did Link seem surprised?"

"Oh no. He has a thing like this happen nearly every evening about this time."

"Don't be brilliant. I mean, did he seem too surprised, as if he knew it all the time? Or did he seem just normally surprised?"

"You don't think Link Simpson has been out shooting, do you, Emily?" Henry asked.

The curtain rose, cutting off further speculation.

Henry hoped Emily wouldn't want to see the show clear through but she expressed horror at the idea of leaving before the end. "After all, Henry," she pointed out, "the tickets were a present. You don't cut off half a tie and send it back at Christmas, do you?"

He was able to sleep a little during the last act, until Emily pinched him. "This isn't the Paramount," she whispered indignantly.

On the way home she insisted that they stop and get him something to eat. Henry didn't feel hungry by this time but he had a sandwich and coffee.

Emily, her mouth full of shrimp salad, suddenly stopped chewing. "Henry," she said, giving him a pathetic wide-eyed look, "I'm afraid to stay alone tonight. If we were married I wouldn't have to."

"You don't have to anyway."

"Save your propositions."

"Suppose we drop you off at the Astor. You can sit in the lobby all night."

Emily looked at him primly. "They've taken out the chairs."

He took her to her apartment, looked in the closets and under the bed, and left her.

He had just turned on a lamp in his own apartment when the phone rang.

"Henry!" It was Emily, frightened. "Somebody's been here. They've moved the brandy. I always keep it inside that French urn thing."

"Where is it now?"

"It's inside the urn, but there are marks in the dust all around the rim. Henry, I'm scared."

"I took the brandy out and had a swallow while you were scrambling the eggs."

"Honestly? You're not just saying that to make me feel better?"

"It's the truth. Now go to bed like a good girl."

Henry took off his tie, absently laid it on the bookcase, and stood staring into space. He had not sampled the brandy in Emily's apartment. Oh well, he told himself, Emily often imagined things. Probably she had made those marks in the dust herself, checking up on the brandy. And suppose someone had been in her apartment—he wouldn't come back again tonight while she was there. If he did, he couldn't get in. Emily's door was locked, and if he knew her, the windows were too.

Aside from asphyxiation, she was in no great danger. He took some quinine and whiskey and got into bed.

After a quarter hour of thinking about the gun, the play, Emily, and his rapidly developing cold, he suddenly sat up.

Maybe he had had a visitor too. He wasn't the sort of person who knew when something had been moved—things were always being moved. He turned on all the lights and roamed around for a half-hour, looking here and there, but he couldn't find undeniable traces of an intruder. He stuck his head out the window, waving a flashlight on the fire escape. There, in the new snow, and now being softly covered by more snow, were footprints. He couldn't believe it at first, and continued to swing the light back and forth as if the marks might disappear. He sneezed, drew in his head, and closed the window. Well, there was no doubt someone had come up the fire escape, and it wasn't the usual route for the milkman. The windows had been locked. It was logical to assume that the visitor had been unable to enter the apartment. Therefore, Henry reasoned, he would be back.

"I hope I'm not here at the time," he said aloud, and feeling a little sheepish, he moved a chest in front of the door, placed all his cooking utensils on the window sill, it being contrary to his principles to sleep without fresh air, and went back to bed.

Chapter 3

THE heat came on with a cheerful whistle and rattle at about half-past eight and Henry, remembering gratefully that it was Sunday, got up and closed the window, looked at himself in the bathroom mirror, decided the cold had a firm grip on his system, drank a glass of milk, took some quinine, and went back to bed.

He had just begun to enjoy the sort of semi-stupor which usually consumed the hours between nine and twelve when the phone rang. If it was Emily he would cut her throat.

It was Emily. "I'm at the studio," she said.

"Why the whisper?"

"I'm afraid they'll hear me."

"Who?"

"They've been here, Henry." Her voice sounded like a tugboat whistle with a shawl over it.

Henry wanted to know why she was in the studio. Emily said she had thought she would finish the screen for Di Nobili. Emily would rather paint than eat, and it was not unusual for her to go over on Sunday and do a job she was interested in. It was very discouraging to be in business with so much energy. Henry never had the slightest urge to enter the studio on a holiday—probably he was lacking in artistic fire.

"What are we going to do?" she asked.

"I suppose I'll have to get dressed."

"You'll have to do more than that, Henry. This is getting serious.

What are they looking for, do you think?"

"I don't know. I don't even care. I've got a cold. Have you had any breakfast?"

"Some. I could have more."

"Meet me in Gottlieb's, half an hour."

He was shaving when Beardsley Satchel came down to borrow two eggs for his wife and a shot of anything at all for himself.

"You alive?" Henry inquired.

"Sure," Satchel said, anxious to tell about it. "You know how I got cut? I couldn't open the door downstairs, so I broke the glass and turned the knob from the inside. I always have trouble with that damned door. I bled a lot, didn't I?"

"You certainly did. Funny the cops haven't been up to look for the mangled body."

"They've been up. They followed the blood to our door. My wife told them she wished they'd take me to jail, but the cop couldn't figure any charge. If I disturbed the peace, he wasn't here to notice it."

Henry, continuing to shave, observed that they might have arrested him for attempted suicide. He hoped Beardsley would go without being put out—if there was anything more boring than Beardsley drunk it was Beardsley sober. The man was completely fascinated by himself and his own behavior. Presently Martha came and got him.

Emily was waiting in Gottlieb's, finishing a cup of coffee and smoking her third cigarette. "I couldn't stay up there. It felt very spooky, Henry. There are so many places where a man could hide. He came in the fire escape and walked all around. I saw the tracks."

"How did they get past all that stuff that's piled against the back window?"

"Pushed, I guess. They really wanted to get in. Di Nobili's mirror is broken. You know what that means, Henry."

"It means Di Nobili is going to be a little sore."

"Speaking of being sore, you should have heard Clarence last night. He called me about one o'clock. We gave him a bust of Sherman to put in a Southern drawing room. He says we've ruined his career. Who was Sherman, Henry?"

Mr. Gottlieb came to wait on them. "We have from Sweden all kinds of new sandwiches," he suggested. "Beautiful."

"I don't want anything that's traveled that far," Henry said. "Scrambled eggs and ham and a couple of honey buns."

"If you have a cold you shouldn't eat all that," Emily pointed out. "I'd like some mince pie, Mr. Gottlieb."

Mr. Gottlieb smiled and surged to the kitchen. He was in love with Emily, but not for herself alone. It was her appetite he admired.

"As soon as we've finished breakfast," Henry announced, "we're going down to the precinct and tell them the whole story."

"Henry! They'll put us in jail for hiding the gun."

"I think I'd feel better in jail. I may as well tell you now, Emily, that I didn't have any of your brandy last night. And somebody came up the fire escape and tried to get in my windows. I don't think they did get in—I usually have the windows locked."

Emily's face fell open. "Henry, they must think we still have the gun."

"Somebody's looking for something. That's all I know. Maybe it's the gun. But how many people want that gun?"

"If the murderer wants it, why didn't he hang on to it in the first place? Stupid, I think."

"He thought he had it hidden in a nice safe place. Mr. Webster's neck. But suddenly Webster comes into the public eye in a big way. He has to get the gun back. Steals Webster from me. Somebody else knows it was in Webster and thinks we took it out and kept it."

Emily looked so worried as Mr. Gottlieb set down her slab of pie that he asked if there was something wrong.

"Mr. Gottlieb," she said, "we have an awful problem. Awful. What would you do if you'd just shot somebody?"

Concern slid through the plump creases in Mr. Gottlieb's face. He looked behind him where three customers were waiting at the cold-cuts counter. "Shh," he begged. "You did this?"

"No. Some friends, we think."

"The guy who hit me was no friend," Henry objected. "We can't tell you about it now, Gottlieb, but you'll be the first to know."

Gottlieb bent forward majestically. "Should it be you go to jail," he said, "I bring in your dinner every Sunday."

"You're a good, kind man," Emily said, giving his mighty hand a pat. "Remember I like my roast beef on the bloody side."

Henry felt better after breakfast, and by the time he and Emily reached the precinct desk in Fifty-first Street he was convinced that the whole thing, including his cold, could be disposed of within a week. He told the officer briefly that they had found a gun and that it had then been stolen.

"Are you making a complaint?" the officer demanded severely.

"No, sir. As I said, the gun was not ours."

"What were you doing with it?"

"It was hidden in our studio in a bust of Daniel Webster."

The sergeant bent a mean eye in Henry's direction. Henry stopped feeling better. "April first is a long way off, son. I'm busy. Good-by."

"Look, sir. I know you're busy, but couldn't you let us talk to someone else? A subordinate. Just a cop. Anybody so we can get this thing off our chests and not feel responsible."

"McNulty!" the sergeant bellowed.

A bulky officer appeared from an inner room. "Yes, sir."

"Take these people inside and listen to them. They want to be listened to."

Henry said "Thanks," and he and Emily followed McNulty into a small room where his game of solitaire was still laid out on a table and his cigar still gave off the smoldering odor of old huaraches.

"What is it you want to talk about?" McNulty inquired politely, offering them chairs.

"We tried to tell the man out there at the desk, Mr. McNulty," Emily said, "but he isn't interested in crime today."

"He's a little off his feed lately," McNulty explained. "He's a good guy. He likes rye."

Henry made a note of the rye. "This is the way it was," he began, "we were patching up the nose of a bust of Daniel Webster—that is, Miss Murdock was. We're in the decorating business. While Miss Murdock was working on the bust, a gun fell out of it."

"Yeah?" McNulty unwrapped a stick of Spearmint, folded it and placed it lovingly on his large pink tongue. "What caliber?"

"I'm not familiar with guns," Henry admitted.

"I see." McNulty eyed him with diminishing respect. "How big was it?"

"About four inches long, I should think. The kind of weapon you might carry around in your pocket or your handbag. Of course it may have been there since the year one—that's what we thought at first.

But when I undertook to deliver the bust to the Belasco Theatre in Forty-fourth Street I was knocked cold and the bust was stolen from me."

McNulty raised an eyebrow. "Hmm," he said profoundly.

"The fact that we know Mrs. Cleo Delaphine, added to the fact that Mrs. Delaphine was so recently shot, made us a little nervous about this incident, and we thought we would get it off our chests and on yours."

"Delaphine?" McNulty repeated without interest. "Never heard of her."

"She was shot night before last," Emily told him. "It's been in all the papers."

"I don't get much time to read." McNulty avoided looking at the cards. "I better take your names."

When Henry gave his the officer showed a glimmer of interest. "There was some trouble in your building. A guy put his arm through a glass door."

"Yes, I reported it."

"You got lots of things to tell us, Mr. Bryce." McNulty eyed Henry's hand-painted tie suspiciously.

"We told Mr. Satchel he ought to have the cut attended to," Emily explained, "but he was so drunk he didn't know he was bleeding."

"What do you want us to do about this gun?" McNulty asked.

"We just thought you might like to know about it if you were working on Mrs. Delaphine's murder, but if you're not on that case—" Henry shrugged.

"You want to report a stolen gun?"

"It wasn't my gun. I don't think I can report it as stolen."

"But you said it was stolen."

"Let's forget the whole thing," Emily suggested. "They don't care about guns here. We've done our duty and reported it."

McNulty nodded. "I think you're right, lady. You don't know the number of the gun, and you don't even know the type of weapon it was, so the report ain't worth a hoot in harrah."

They left him to go back to his game, but Henry thought he detected a glimmer of concern in McNulty's placid blue eye as he watched them go. The officer at the desk did not look up as they went out.

"Is that the kind of protection we have around here?" Emily demanded outside.

"Not so loud. We don't want them down on us."

"They wouldn't get out of their chairs for anything less than a World Series. The idea! How would we know what caliber gun it was unless we were criminals?" She stopped suddenly. "We forgot to tell him our apartments had been broken into."

"Well, we're not going back. He'd ask if anything was stolen, and if it wasn't he'd want to know what we were complaining about. We ought to be glad to have a little company."

"I always thought it would be exciting to know somebody who got shot. It isn't at all. Nobody cares, do they?" Emily wiped her nose sadly on a piece of Kleenex and stopped to read the Sunday *Tribune* on a newsstand, although she had the same paper at home. "Fair and colder," she said. "I guess we can't paint my kitchen this winter. Do you want me to help you put the things back in yours?"

"God forbid. I'd never find anything."

"I can't come over, even?"

"I suppose you can, for a little while. But it's an awful mess. I don't know why you want to."

Emily smiled sweetly. "I like to be near you, Henry. I feel sad today. Do you think I'm getting appendicitis?"

Emily always thought she was getting something. He didn't pay any attention to her internal disturbances. They had to pass the studio entrance and Link's shop, on their way up to Sixty-second Street. Henry paused to look in Link's window.

"The door's open," Emily said, surprised. "Why, there's Link!"

Link jumped up from his desk when he saw them and came out. "Where the devil have you been? I've been ringing your apartment for an hour and a half."

"Anything wrong?" Henry asked, thinking that Simpson looked like the eighth year of a raccoon coat.

"Somebody tried to break into the shop last night."

"What's so amazing about that?" Henry asked. "You've had people break in before."

Link deflated somewhat. "You don't think it had anything to do with the gun?"

"Of course it did," Emily said. "Henry's just being superior. The studio was broken into, from the fire escape. We have to leave the windows open on account of the paint—it might blow up, and even if it didn't blow up the smell would knock you over in the morning if you had everything tight shut all night. So that's how they got in, and walked around and looked everywhere. Muddy tracks. They had snow on their feet, and there's plenty of dust on our floors to make mud. And I found prints on the fire escape in the snow. Isn't that something? And not only that, but they tried to get into Henry's apartment, and they did get into mine."

"No fooling?" Link's long, lean face assumed the pointed expression of a bird dog on the trot. "What are they looking for?"

Henry shrugged. "You've got me, brother. You'd think the gun would have satisfied him. Or her. I wonder what he did with the bust of Daniel. That's going to be a little inconvenient to dispose of, isn't it?"

Link didn't see why he couldn't just drop it in a city trash can.

"I'm cold," Emily complained, jigging from one foot to the other. "Let's go up to your apartment, Henry."

While they were waiting for Link to close the shop Henry glanced up at the windows of the Thinkers' Club across the street. There was the rotund little man whom he had noticed on Saturday, the one who had taken the pill. As Henry looked, the man's eyes shifted downward, caught Emily and himself, remained on them. Perhaps, since they were the only people in view at the moment, it was natural that the little man should stare at them, but he did seem to take an unusual interest. Then Link came out, and Henry forgot about the fellow.

The radiator was cold in Henry's apartment when they got there. New York janitors operated on the theory that if you gave the tenants a burst of heat in the morning you could let them congeal slowly until about six. All janitors lived at least ten blocks from the buildings they tended, to discourage complaints.

"I haven't seen a cockroach since we painted," Henry was saying, when there was a loud knock at the door. He opened it for a bulky man in a black overcoat.

"A Mr. Henry Bryce live here?" he demanded.

"You're looking at him," Henry said. "Come in."

The man took two strides to the center of the room. "I'm Burgreen, Seventeenth Precinct, working on the Delaphine case. Do I smell paint? Paint's what I'm looking for. Where is it?" He stuck his head into the kitchen. "Red. Good. Red is what we want." He glanced at Emily, who was looking unusually small and shy on the sofa, and at Link, then he asked Henry, "Were you in Mrs. Delaphine's apartment Friday night?"

"No," Henry said, puzzled.

Burgreen turned to Emily. She was a bright crimson and she was lighting a cigarette with intense concentration. "You're in the decorating business too?"

"How did you know?" She gave him one of her wide, trusting smiles.

"Your dirty hands." Burgreen referred to a scribbled envelope. "Are you Miss Emily Murdock? Did you go to the Delaphine house on Friday night?"

"One at a time, please," Emily begged, the smile becoming slightly hardened.

"Even you decorators must know your own names."

"She does," Henry put in gently. "She's a little slow mentally. Give her time and she'll respond."

"Mr. Burgreen, have you met our friend Lincoln Simpson? He's in the antique business. Very prominent, awfully successful. Sells to the best people."

Link grinned. "I don't imagine Mr. Burgreen is interested in the antique business, Emily."

"I am." He went over Link like a gardener with a rake. "We will take up Mr. Simpson later. Now I would like an answer to my second question, Miss Murdock." He sat down, staring at her with his amiable blue eyes.

"You mean did I go to see Mrs. Delaphine before she was murdered? I was there for lunch that day. We had lettuce sandwiches and milk."

"Is that so? And you were engaged at that time in painting Mr. Bryce's kitchen?"

"No," Emily admitted. "We did that later, that same night."

"The night Mrs. Delaphine was murdered, in other words?"

Link interrupted. "I think it would be fairer, Mr. Burgreen, if you would tell us what you're trying to find out."

"My object is not to be fair, but to get information," Burgreen grunted. "However, I don't mind saying that we found red paint, slightly tacky, on the outside door and on the door from the foyer to the living room of Mrs. Delaphine's house. This paint was observed when we were notified of the death and went there to examine the premises yesterday morning."

"Oh, but, Mr. Burgreen, I did some work for Mrs. Delaphine when I was there to lunch. I painted some niches for her."

"Red?"

Emily hesitated briefly. "I generally use some red in everything."

"Would the paint you smeared on a doorknob at noon be tacky the next morning?"

Henry interrupted to say that was quite possible in this damp winter weather.

Burgreen stood up. "If you don't mind, let's go over there now, Miss Murdock, and you can show me what you painted red in Mrs. Delaphine's house."

Emily sighed. "I give up. I didn't use any red paint. The niches are gold with white striping."

Henry, who stood behind Burgreen, caught Emily's eye and shook his head.

"All right, Henry," Emily said, "I won't tell him anything."

"I think, Bryce," Burgreen said dryly, "we'll get along faster if you don't try to help." He took an old brown pipe from his pocket, began packing it with tobacco from a green-and-white package labeled Galvin's Irish Mixture.

"Now, Miss Murdock, you were in Mrs. Delaphine's house the night she was murdered, weren't you?"

Emily swallowed. "I was there."

"Oh, Lord," Link groaned, settling back on the sofa, his long, thin hands folded on his stomach, his eyes half closed as he watched the detective.

"You don't have to answer these questions, Emily," Henry told her. "We'll get a lawyer."

"He'll find out anyway," Emily sighed. "You can see by looking at him that he gets to know everything without much trouble. Even his overcoat is sharp along the edges. I had to go to Cleo's."

"What for?" Henry demanded.

"I left my ring there. The tourmaline you gave me. I knew you'd be mad, so I said I was going to my place for another brush and a head-ache tablet, and instead I went to Mrs. Delaphine's and got my ring."

Burgreen looked pleased. "Was the lady alive?"

"Oh yes," Emily said cheerfully. "She gave me the ring herself."

"Was she nervous or upset?"

"She didn't seem to be. No, I think she was rather pleased over something."

Burgreen asked if Emily had seen anyone else there, or had noticed anyone in the street, and Emily said no.

"Now about this gun," Burgreen went on. "McNulty says you came into the station this morning with a weird story about a gun falling out of a bust of Daniel Webster. As I already had your names on my list in connection with the death of Mrs. Delaphine, I found the information interesting."

"You mean you have us down as suspects?" Emily cried.

"Don't be alarmed, Miss Murdock. Let's hear how a weapon happened to be in a plaster bust."

Emily sat forward eagerly but Henry silenced her. "Let me tell it. You'll have us both in jail. Clarence Mould, a friend of Emily's, called up yesterday afternoon and asked if Emily still had the bust of Daniel Webster, and if she would be willing to rent it for a few days. Clarence needed it for the set of a play, which was opening last night. He said he'd had a bust, but somebody broke it. So Emily agreed to deliver the one we had to the theater."

"How did this Mr. Mould know you had a bust of Daniel Webster?" Burgreen inquired.

"Most of our friends knew about it. Mrs. Giddings' bust was a sort of standing joke. Emily had promised to repair and deliver it within a week. Three years ago."

Burgreen picked a thread off his knee and dropped it on the rug. "Did Clarence Mould know Mrs. Delaphine?"

They didn't think so. "Clarence isn't a bit social." Emily added.

"When Emily started patching up the bust," Henry went on, "the gun fell out of it."

"I screamed," Emily added proudly.

"Then you called the police and reported the finding of a weapon," Burgreen suggested.

"Oh no," she said. "When you do that you have to spend the night in jail. That's what happened to a woman in my mother's block in Babylon. It was awful because she has a gallbladder condition."

Burgreen wanted to know where she had heard such a bunch of nonsense. "Never mind," he said, "you didn't report the weapon when you found it. What did you do with it?"

"Emily wired it inside the bust," Henry told him. "I was to deliver it to Mould at the Belasco. I stepped out of the cab in Forty-fourth Street, someone hit me on the head, and when I came to the bust was gone. That's all."

"That isn't all," Emily protested. "Henry and I went to the play— Clarence had given us seats for the opening—and while we were there somebody got into my apartment and looked all through it, and somebody tried to get into Henry's but he doesn't think they succeeded, and they were in the studio too. This morning I found tracks all over the place. It's easy to get into the studio from the fire escape because we leave the back windows open on account of explosions."

"What kind of gun was it?" Burgreen asked Henry.

"I don't know," Henry admitted, embarrassed. "Guns aren't in my line."

Burgreen looked as if he didn't believe anyone could be so ignorant. "We're looking for a .25 Colt automatic. Oddly enough, we find that Mrs. Lord has a permit for a .25 Colt automatic."

Henry looked at him sharply. "Couldn't she show you her gun?"

"She doesn't know where it is. Now isn't that a coincidence?"

"Perhaps James knows," Henry suggested uneasily.

Burgreen smiled. "Quite right. Mr. Lord, being a perfect gentleman and obviously fond of your sister, says he threw the gun away. Imagine that."

"Maybe he did."

"Maybe. But if, as he claims, he dropped it in a trash can, it ought to have turned up. He says Mrs. Lord obtained the gun without his knowledge, and when he saw it he was alarmed. She has a habit, it seems, of staging near-suicides. So he disposed of the weapon. Excellent story."

"Beansie usually tells the truth," Emily put in. "You'd better believe him, Mr. Burgreen."

"Oh, I believe him absolutely," Burgreen said. "Of course he may have shot Mrs. Delaphine himself with his wife's gun, in which case his story is a great convenience."

Emily studied him gravely. "You know I like you, Mr. Burgreen."

"Thank you, ma'am."

"But I don't think you're very bright. Not if you actually believe Mr. Lord killed Cleo Delaphine."

Burgreen smiled. "I know what you mean. I've seen Lord and he's plainly a man of great kindness and wouldn't stick a pin in a butterfly. But I also know the Seventeenth Precinct, Miss Murdock. Anybody can be a murderer around here. Sometimes I wonder if it's the strange things you decorators make them live with."

"I take it you've seen Cornelia's apartment," Link remarked. "Di Nobili did that. He says it reflects her personality."

Emily asked the detective if he had noticed the serpent climbing the wall. "That's Cornelia," she explained, "and the little green parakeet is James."

"Di Nobili has no imagination," Link muttered. "I think of James and Cornelia as the walrus and the mermaid. Anyway, Burgreen, you can't blame it all on the decorators. If these people weren't a little odd to begin with they wouldn't live around here. Emily forgot to mention that my shop was broken into last night. It appears that someone is looking for something, presumably the gun. But if they took the gun from Henry, why are they still looking for it?"

"It's two different people," Emily suggested.

Burgreen was not interested in their speculations. He asked some questions about Mrs. Delaphine and they told him what they could.

"James or Cornelia could tell you more about her," Henry pointed out. "They were friends."

"Cornelia and Mrs. Delaphine were hating friends," Emily corrected.

Henry thought that was too strong. "They enjoyed bickering," he said. "Nothing serious. A game they played."

"What about Mrs. Delaphine's ex-husband, this analyst fellow?" Burgreen asked.

"Harmon is awfully nice," Emily volunteered. "He never was the least bit of trouble when we were doing work for his wife. He thought it would take her mind off herself to have a lot of decorating done. I guess it was amusing for her but it was just hell for us."

"Hell?" Burgreen appeared surprised that such a word should have come out of Emily's pink-and-white face. "In what way?"

"She was patronizing and indecisive," Link put in, "and besides, she didn't pay her bills."

"I imagine Harmon is just plain glad she's dead," Emily told Burgreen. "She pestered the life out of him, even after they were divorced, Cornelia said. She wanted him back. Harmon was too smart for that. Isn't it funny how analysts always marry cases?"

Burgreen looked interested. "You think Mrs. Delaphine wanted her husband back?"

"Of course," Emily said. "She didn't have anybody else, and every woman needs at least one husband. Especially at her age."

"You have a husband, Miss Murdock?" he inquired casually.

"No. Are you married?"

Burgreen was caught off guard. He said hastily, "You knew, of course, that Mrs. Delaphine tried to telephone someone before she died?"

"No!" Emily gasped. "That wasn't in the *Mirror*."

"One for our side," Burgreen grunted.

Henry wondered how long the detective was going to stay. His pipe was going out.

"Who did she call?" Link inquired, his eyes not quite so listless.

The detective said that was what he would like to know. He waved away Henry's proffered lighter, took a handful of kitchen matches from his pocket, and drew on the pipe. "Who would you say she would be most likely to call?"

Link shrugged. "If I'd just been shot I'd call the police."

"She didn't do that," Burgreen told him. "Or if she did try to call us, she died before the call was completed. No record of anything. The question is, was she successful in reaching someone else?"

Henry objected. "If she got hold of somebody they'd naturally call the police, wouldn't they?"

Burgreen shook his head. "Depends."

"You mean maybe she called the person who shot her?" Emily asked, shuddering.

"Possible." Burgreen stood up abruptly. "However, she was shot from fairly close range, as she faced the killer, so she may have seen him. McNulty's waiting for me in her house. Doing a little more work over there." He knocked the coals from his pipe into the fireplace, thereby igniting an accumulation of papers and trash, and opened the door.

"I know it's a little unusual, but do you mind if I go along?" Henry asked. "I could identify the red paint on the doorknobs."

Burgreen looked at him a minute. "Why not?" he said.

"I'm going, too, then." Emily jumped up.

"Oh no. No, Miss Murdock." Burgreen was firm.

"Why not?"

"Can't have the place cluttered up with a lot of females."

"I liked you at first," she said sulkily. "Oh well, Henry tells me every-thing."

Henry followed Mr. Burgreen outside and up the steps of Mrs. Delaphine's blue stucco house next door. McNulty was sitting gloomily on a brocade chair in the living room, eating a chocolate bar and reading the Sunday comics. "Geez, I thought you was never gonna get here," he grunted. "I turned up the heat."

"Bryce, did you have any particular reason for wanting to come with me?" Burgreen asked.

Henry shook his head. "After you've found a gun and been knocked out and had your working quarters searched by an unknown trespasser, you develop a mild curiosity."

"I see. Well, look around. It's a nice place."

Henry sat down and watched Burgreen going through papers in a desk and a table. It was a tedious job. McNulty fell asleep.

"I don't like a case like this," Burgreen volunteered after a while. "You can't use the usual channels of information."

"Meaning?"

"Most crimes we solve with the help of informers. A jewel robbery, for instance, can be boiled down to a given circle of characters. When a lady is murdered by a friend, there are no informers. Naturally we question her ex-husband. But we've got nothing actually pinned on the guy, so far. That character who lives over you—Satchel—had an ap-pointment with her on Friday. Notation on her calendar. But from the report on him for Friday night, I don't think he was in any shape to fire a straight shot. He says he did not have an appointment with her, by the way."

"Maybe he couldn't remember," Henry suggested. "Any paint on his clothes?"

Burgreen looked at him sharply. "Yes," he said. "There was."

"Do you have the garment?"

"We do."

"Mind if we look at it sometime?"

Burgreen wanted to know what for.

"Emily is a wizard with paint."

"I see. I'll bring it to your studio." He returned to the letters and bank statements. Suddenly he sat up. "Something comes to light."

Henry waited impatiently while Burgreen read a letter on cheap blue notepaper. The detective folded it and put it in his pocket.

"Secret and confidential?" Henry asked.

"I guess not." Burgreen handed him the note.

It was poorly written, in pencil. "Cleo. See you Friday night, Donald Clark," it read.

"Ever hear of a Donald Clark in her life?" Burgreen demanded.

Henry shook his head. "Better ask someone who really knew her." Burgreen referred to one of his pink cards. "Hmm. Her maiden name was Clark," he said. "More footwork."

Henry followed the detective and McNulty through the house, noting a lot of Unity literature in the bedroom and some manuals on handwriting, and a dozen works of psychology and psychiatry, possibly left there by Harmon.

"She liked to think about herself," Burgreen remarked, also reading these titles. The number of hats in her closet shocked him. "Don't ever get married, McNulty," he said.

"Your advice is twenty years too late," McNulty said sadly. "What about me takin' home a couple of them hats?"

"You want your wife to develop a taste for fifty-dollar millinery?"

Henry didn't go back to his apartment when he left Burgreen. Instead, he walked down Lexington Avenue to Fifty-fifth Street and rang his sister's bell.

James let him in. "She's edgy," he said in a low voice as he hung Henry's overcoat in the closet in the foyer. "You won't say anything to upset her?"

Henry entered the living room, where Di Nobili had freely spent Lord's money to attain an effect of impending doom. Cornelia was stretched barefoot on a blood-red sofa, holding a glass on her stomach and staring at the ceiling. She didn't look at him.

"Aren't you starting early?" Henry asked sternly.

"Oh, shut up."

"She's been very good lately," James put in. "A drink before dinner won't hurt her."

"I hear your gun has conveniently disappeared," Henry went on, ignoring James.

"What interest can that possibly have for you, my dear brother?"

Henry sat down. "If you wanted to shoot Cleo, why didn't you do it with somebody else's gun?"

"You're such an ass, Henry. I didn't shoot Cleo."

"Of course she didn't," James said firmly. "You know Cornelia well enough for that." His smile, Henry thought as he watched James lower himself stiffly into a deep chair, was a little anxious. He had the feeling that James was on edge, and this suspicion was confirmed when the telephone rang. James jumped to answer it.

"Yes," he said quickly, and listened. "I believe she did some business with his firm at one time. But whether she had continued the connection, I don't know. You could of course find out from the company itself. About the other fellow, I never heard her mention him." He put the phone down. "That was Burgreen. Wanted to know if Cleo had been doing business with Beardsley Satchel. Why should he ask me? Cornelia, did you ever hear Cleo mention anyone named Clark—Donald Clark?"

Cornelia shook her head. "The whole thing is childish," she murmured, finishing her drink. "Get me another short one, Beansie, like a darling."

James, with an apologetic glance at Henry, went to the small pantry and did as he was told.

"How long since you've seen your gun?" Henry demanded, facing his sister.

"How do I know? I didn't take it out and look at it every day. I got it as a joke, really."

"Who helped you get it?"

"No one. They gave me a permit without any trouble. I said I needed it for protection. Your friend Link Simpson gave me the idea—he was telling about the fun some friend of his had getting a gun permit, so I thought I'd try it myself. But I've had the thing for nearly a year, Henry. You can't possibly tie it up with an intention to murder poor old Cleo." She opened her large cruel eyes very wide and laughed at him. She had a most unpleasant laugh. "You love playing policeman, don't you, dear? And Emily must be simply wallowing in it. Although I don't suppose she understands what's going on, really."

James came back, handed Henry a drink. "Have dinner with us, old boy," he offered. "We're just going round the corner."

Henry thanked him, said no. He felt that James wanted his company, perhaps even his help. There was something pathetic in the way he accepted the refusal. Henry didn't want to spend any more time with his sister, and as soon as the drink was down he left them.

On Monday morning, before Henry had his brushes out, Mrs. Cormorant telephoned. "Mr. Bryce," she shouted in her great booming voice, "I must say I am horribly disappointed in you. I know one cannot rely on Miss Murdock, but I thought you were different!"

"What's the trouble, Mrs. Cormorant?" Henry asked wearily. "Something wrong with the bird cage?"

"Wrong? You know perfectly well I didn't get the bird cage."

"But it went out to you Saturday evening." Henry turned to Emily. "Mrs. Cormorant says she didn't get the bird cage. Roscoe delivered it, didn't he?"

"He took it with him. Tell her we'll call her back."

Henry disengaged himself from the angry voice, promised to call back.

"Roscoe ought to be here," Emily complained. "He gets worse and worse. I'll have to fire him again."

Ten minutes later Roscoe came in, looking sheepish and wearing a bandage around his head.

"What happened to you?" Henry demanded.

"Nothing."

Henry reached over and felt Roscoe's skull. Roscoe jumped. "Somebody hit you." Henry accused.

"Yes, boss."

Emily sat down, looking frightened. "None of us are safe. Roscoe, who did it? Where were you?"

"What about the bird cage, first?" Henry interrupted. "Mrs. Cormorant says she didn't get it."

Roscoe spread out his hands, shrugged. "I tell everything. If not, you find out anyway."

"You're right. What happened?"

"First, I do not take the bird cage. You take the bird cage."

"I?" Henry repeated stupidly.

"I take man's head with gun inside. Give you bird cage."

"By mistake?"

"No. I think I will hide this gun."

Emily sat forward. "That's why they went on looking for the gun after they slugged you, Henry. They didn't get it from you because you didn't have it."

"So," Roscoe drew a deep sigh, "I take man's head home, put package under bed, and I worry. What they do to Roscoe, I wonder, when they come find gun under Roscoe's bed?"

"You dope," Emily said. "Why didn't you throw the gun down the sewer?"

"The Sanitations have already enough trouble, Miss Murdock."

"But why did you want to take it home with you? Henry was getting rid of it."

"Police very smart, Miss Murdock. Find gun in man's head in theater, say, 'Miss Murdock put gun here. Arrest Miss Murdock. To jail. To chair. No more Miss Murdock. Roscoe, no job. Roscoe sorry about everything.' "

"Where's the gun now?"

Roscoe shook his head. "Who knows? Sunday after dinner am I sitting in room, frowning. Comes phone call. Comes lady yelling up to Roscoe, 'Roscoe, come to phone.' I go. Somebody say Miss Murdock in big trouble. She need gun back. If no gun, police take away Miss Murdock."

"Who said this?" Emily demanded. "Was it a man or a woman?"

"I say a man. Maybe not. Maybe lady with big voice?"

"Go on," Henry begged. "What did you do?"

"First I say cannot bring gun. Do not have gun. Then he say, 'Okay, Miss Murdock hang.' So I say where to bring gun? He say Nineteen Street and Third Avenue. I say, 'You want me bring man's head, too?' and he say, 'No, no. Just gun.' "

"And when you got there he knocked you out?"

Roscoe smiled. "You know," he said. "First nobody there. Then somebody come up quick behind Roscoe, bang on head, Roscoe down on sidewalk. Very bad fall, skin nose. See?"

"We see," Emily said. "He took the gun, of course."

"Guess so. I sit up on sidewalk, and bum come along and say, 'Bud, you gotta dime?' and I say, 'Sure,' and I give him dime, and he goes away. So after a while I get up and go home."

"Poor Roscoe," Emily said. "How do you feel now?"

"Good." He smiled. "Was not such a strong fellah hit me."

They gave him a bed to paint blue, and he settled down contentedly. Henry thought they ought to tell Burgreen what had happened. Emily argued that it would be more fun to see if he found it out for himself.

"After all, Emily," Henry pointed out, "this is not a game he's playing. He'll be a little irritated with us when he does find out, if we don't tell him. In fact he may suspect us."

"I'm sure he suspects us anyway," Emily said. "He's supposed to suspect everybody."

Henry had already dialed a number, and was asking for Mr. Burgreen. He was not in the detectives' room at the station. Henry left a message.

Emily's mother called from Babylon. "Emily," she said, "I wish you'd move out of that dreadful neighborhood. There's been a murder, right in your street."

"Yes, Mother," Emily said, pleased that the news had gotten clear to Babylon. "She's the woman who didn't take me to lunch on Friday. Isn't that nice?"

"I think you should move."

"I can't, right in the middle of everything. They'd be sure I killed her. Anyway, Henry wouldn't leave Sixty-second Street."

"You'd be far better off without that man," Mrs. Murdock snapped.

Emily said, "Yes, Mother. I'll call you later in the week."

At half-past eleven Mr. Burgreen walked into the studio carrying a green overcoat, not his own.

"What a mess," he said, looking around.

"You should have seen it a month ago," Emily answered. "Sit down."

"I wouldn't dare. You wanted to see me?"

Henry, with interruptions from Emily and Roscoe, told him about the gun. Burgreen asked Roscoe questions, but Henry didn't think he got any leads as to the identity of the person who had stolen the gun. Roscoe tried to imitate the voice he had heard on the phone, but he sounded more like a parrot with a sore throat than any of their acquaintance.

Burgreen took out a notebook, glanced doubtfully at the chair which Emily had offered him, sat down, and stretched his feet under a nest of Chinese tables. "I need help," he said briskly. "If this gun which keeps raising welts on the members of the Lentement decorating establishment is the same gun which killed Mrs. Delaphine, then it must have arrived here on the person of one of your visitors. It must have been placed inside Mr. Webster on Saturday, presumably before you knew you were going to rent the bust to the theater."

"Why?" Emily asked.

Henry patiently pointed out that whoever hid the weapon thought it wouldn't be disturbed.

Burgreen tolerated the interruption, continued, "Who was here on Saturday, before you started to repair the bust?"

"My word," Emily said, "everybody was here. We had people all day long—Di Nobili, Perkins, that awful woman with the cuckoo clock, Mr. Means for the shutters, three different truckmen, the man to fix the dripping faucet, the man to deliver the Great Bear spring water, and of course everybody who wanted to talk about the murder."

Burgreen said he wasn't interested in the man who delivered the Great Bear spring water. "Who came to talk about the murder?"

"Cornelia," Emily said promptly and with malice.

"Your sister, by the way"—Burgreen turned to Henry—"has a key to Mrs. Delaphine's house. Why?"

"They were friendly, in a hostile sort of way."

"She has used the key."

"Is that so?" Henry regarded the detective thoughtfully. "It wouldn't seem sensible, if she killed Cleo Delaphine, to go back into Cleo's house."

"Is your sister a sensible woman, Mr. Bryce?"

Emily smiled. "She's a very odd job, Mr. Burgreen. She jumps out of planes."

"Troublemaker," Roscoe added. "No damn good."

Burgreen said he knew all that. "Who else was here on Saturday?"

"James, of course," Emily told him.

Burgreen stared into space, took out his pipe. "There was a strong friendship between Mr. Lord and the late Mrs. Delaphine? They were often together, I understand."

Henry said it was a friendship of long standing, perhaps twenty years.

"Delaphine wasn't in love with your sister's husband?"

Emily laughed. "What an idea!"

The detective scowled at her. "I was trying out the idea of jealousy between Mrs. Delaphine and Cornelia Lord. Both, I gather, are extremely emotional, spoiled, grasping."

"He's been talking to Harmon," Emily suggested. "Does Harmon think Cornelia killed Mrs. Delaphine?"

Burgreen didn't answer. "Who else was here?"

"Harmon," Henry said. "And that's all, as far as friends of Cleo Delaphine are concerned. The other people Emily named are business associates. Of course Link Simpson was in and out, but he doesn't count."

Burgreen raised an eyebrow. He didn't say anything, but Emily argued with his silence. "Link hates guns," she said. "Besides, he's a vegetarian."

"Simpson was almost immediately aware, wasn't he, that you were going to rent the bust to the theater?" Burgreen asked.

"That's so." Emily looked troubled. "Link was the first person to know that."

Henry told Burgreen he thought it was a waste of time to consider Link—he was a gentle guy with a strong sense of justice. "How do you know the gun was hidden here on Saturday?" he challenged. "Why couldn't the murderer have come into the studio on Friday night by way of the fire escape?"

Emily reminded him that there weren't any tracks on the floor on Saturday morning.

"It didn't snow on Friday night," Henry said. "His feet were dry."

"Miss Murdock," Burgreen interrupted, "take a look at this overcoat, will you? It has some red paint on it. I'd like to know if it's the kind of paint you were using on Bryce's kitchen."

Emily bent over the sleeve, examined the stiff stains. She scrambled through the worktable drawer for a reading glass, took the coat to the light. "It's pigment," she decided. "Pure, dried-up pigment."

"You mean it isn't wall paint?" Burgreen demanded.

"No," Emily said. "It's coloring."

"Is she right?" Burgreen asked Henry.

"Better take her word for it. On any other subject I'd rather believe an intelligent horse, but on paint—Emily knows."

Burgreen looked puzzled. "Would a person entering Mrs. Delaphine's house after you had been there, daubing things up with your paint-smeared hands and smock, Miss Murdock, have picked up any of this pure pigment?"

"We did add some coloring to the paint, but I don't think it got on me, did it, Henry? I just squeezed it out of the tube into the bucket. Wait." She walked to a cluttered wooden box, took out a lead tube and with a penknife scraped some of the dried pigment from around the cap onto the worktable. "See if it's the same."

Henry and Burgreen looked at it. "You've got something. It isn't the same shade," Henry exclaimed. "Whose coat is it?"

"Beardsley Satchel's."

"Beardsley?" Emily's blue eyes popped. "How would Beardsley get into any paint?"

"I don't believe he did," Burgreen volunteered. "Someone not as familiar as you are with paints planted this bit of coloring on Satchel."

"Why?"

"To make it look as if Satchel had been in Mrs. Delaphine's house after you were there, Miss Murdock."

"Oh." Emily reflected on this. "That isn't very nice, is it?"

"Didn't you say Satchel had an appointment with Mrs. Delaphine on Friday night?" Henry asked, remembering.

"There was a note on her calendar."

"But you think it may have been planted?"

"Anyone can call up and say, 'This is Satchel, I'm coming over to see you Friday night if it's all right with you.' So Delaphine writes it down on her calendar. No trace of the person who made the call."

"Have you found out anything about Donald Clark—fellow who wrote Delaphine that he would be there on Friday?"

Burgreen shook his head. "No such name turns up, so far."

Chapter 4

IT WAS on Wednesday that Henry again noticed the little man at the window of the Thinkers' Club. He was standing with his vest against the pane—his stomach was his most protuberant point—and staring fixedly across the avenue at the windows of the studio.

At first Henry thought the man was merely staring while he thought of something else, but he went away, came back, pulled up an armchair, held a magazine, and continued to fix his eyes on the windows of the Lentement studio.

Emily hadn't noticed and Henry did not call her attention to him. Ordinarily he would have extracted entertainment from a thing of this kind but there was something vaguely disturbing about the fellow. Those fixed little eyes annoyed him. He moved the table he was painting so he wouldn't have to face the windows.

"What's the matter, Henry?" Emily demanded. "You're fidgety as a dead cat."

"Nothing."

"You'd better eat more fresh vegetables."

"Anything you say, dear."

It was Roscoe who gave it away. He was always looking out the windows, and if he saw something which struck a note in his peculiar brain he mentioned it. "There he is again," he said, pointing his dripping brush in the direction of the Thinkers' Club.

"Who?" Emily didn't look up.

"The guy with the eyes."

The little man must have perceived that his vigil was noticed. He hastily left the window. Emily glanced across briefly but didn't see anybody.

"He looks and he looks," Roscoe said. "I see him every day."

"The Thinkers' Club is full of odd jobs," Emily pointed out. "Why does James want to belong to a thing like that? All they do is try to forget Roosevelt. Negative, I call it."

"James likes to have some place to go when Cornelia is being difficult," Henry suggested. "Anyway, they're his type."

"If he likes it, he can have it. I wouldn't belong."

"They wouldn't want you. Men only. If I ever marry you—which Heaven forbid—I'll join the Thinkers' Club myself, as a refuge. Harmon used to go there, too, to get away from Cleo."

Emily pursed her lips and painted a white rosebud on a dark green chest. "I wish Mr. Burgreen would come back." She looked up eagerly as someone knocked at the metal door.

Roscoe let in a messenger with a very large box from the Waldorf-Astoria Florist addressed to Miss Emily Murdock.

"For me?" Emily looked at the box uncertainly. "It can't be for me. There's a mistake. You'd better take it back."

"Nonsense." Henry accepted the box and the messenger left.

"Do you really think it's for me?" Emily asked.

"Of course it's for you, stupid. If you don't open it, I will."

She ripped off the string, lifted the lid, and revealed enough red roses for a horse's grave. Emily sat down. "I don't believe it. Nobody would send me roses."

"Some poor dope evidently did. How about reading the card?"

Emily looked at Henry with dawning hope. "Henry, you didn't——"

"No. Sorry. My money's too valuable to throw away on women."

She sighed, took the card out of the envelope.

" 'To a lovely lady, from a friend,' " Henry read. "That's very illuminating. Have you a friend, Emily?"

Roscoe, who had been studying the box, said suddenly, "Maybe not good. Maybe blow up."

"Oh, Roscoe," Emily protested. "Don't you think anybody would want to be nice to me?"

"Sure, Miss Murdock. But be careful."

Henry took the flowers out of the box and put them in a bucket of water. Nothing happened. Apparently the gift was genuine.

Emily phoned Link and asked him if he'd sent the roses. Link had not. "Maybe Clarence Mould did," he suggested, "although he was awfully sore about Sherman."

Clarence, when they called him, denied any knowledge of the flowers.

"It must be somebody I don't know, but why would they send me a present?" Emily wondered. "It makes me nervous. I like to know who and why."

At intervals during the afternoon she buried her nose in the roses, examined the card, and stared thoughtfully into space. "Henry," she pleaded, "why didn't you send them?"

"Because somebody else did. You ought to be glad you have a sincere admirer."

"I'm not. I just want you to admire me."

"I know you too well. However, I'll take you to dinner if you like."

It was a rather wearing evening. When something puzzled Emily she couldn't let it alone, she worried it to shreds. She went over the list of all the men she had ever known—it was quite a list—and by the time they reached dessert Emily was back in the fourth grade, musing over a towhead named Albert. Henry took her to a movie to distract her, but she went right on thinking about the flowers, and the last thing she said when he left her at her door was, "If you think of anybody during the night, will you call me?"

"Oh, sure," he promised.

When Henry reached the studio in the morning Roscoe was there— he had his own key. He hadn't been so early in months. "What's the matter?" Henry asked. Then he saw the roses. They were completely pulverized, chopped up like spinach all over the worktable.

"Emily's going to fire you, Roscoe," he said.

"I do it for Miss Murdock. Something wrong with them roses."

"Did you find anything wrong?"

"Maybe they poison her."

"Did they poison you?"

Roscoe shrugged. "I don't poison easy."

Emily was incensed. She fired Roscoe. He went out for a cup of coffee and came back and hired himself again. Henry tried to pacify her. "He's protecting you, Emily. He reads all this murder stuff and you know how his mind works, if you can call it working. You have to make allowances."

"Oh, all right. But you don't know how it feels, having your only two dozen roses made into salad."

At lunchtime Henry, with apologies to his better judgment, stopped in at Piecoli's and ordered a dozen pink rosebuds.

The flowers and Mr. Burgreen arrived at the same moment. This was not exactly what Henry had planned.

Emily cleared a chair for the police officer and then opened the box. She blushed. "Oh, Mr. Burgreen. I never dreamed it was you!"

Henry cleared his throat and decided to let it ride.

"What goes on?" Burgreen growled.

"You sent the red roses, too, didn't you?" Emily beamed.

"What red roses? I came up to ask you about some more paint. We scraped this off another overcoat." He took an envelope from his pocket and handed it to Henry.

"You didn't send the flowers?" Emily persisted.

"Do I go around ordering flowers for my suspects?" Burgreen grunted. "What's the matter with her?"

"She's bewildered by an admirer," Henry explained. "Emily, I sent the pink roses. Not from the Waldorf, by the way."

"Why didn't you say so? There's nobody I'd rather have flowers from."

Burgreen cleared his throat impatiently. "If you could just give me a minute of your time, Miss Murdock."

"Oh, certainly. Any amount." Emily gazed at him with her mouth open.

"Is that the paint you were using in Bryce's kitchen, or is it some more pigment?" Burgreen demanded.

Emily looked at it carefully. "It's paint," she decided. "Where did it come from?"

"You mean it's the kind of paint you were using Friday night?"

"I guess so. Don't you think so, Henry?"

Henry said it looked like the same paint—they could take it over to his apartment and compare it if Burgreen liked. The detective hesitated. "It came off James Lord's overcoat," he said.

"Then you don't need to worry about it," Henry told him. "Lord was in my apartment while we were painting and he got paint on himself. Emily helped him clean it off. She missed some, as usual."

Emily confirmed this statement, in detail, and while she and Burgreen were talking Henry glanced across the avenue.

There was that little man again, standing near the window of the Thinkers' Club, his small body half concealed by the tasseled draperies, his eyes fixed intently on the windows of the studio. Henry stared back, and the little man moved uneasily, pretended to look at his watch, and when Henry did not drop his eyes, finally turned away and disappeared. Who the devil was he, and why this absorbing interest in the Lentement studio? Henry decided to ask James about him—he didn't like the look of the fellow. Something occurred to him.

"Burgreen, you haven't a man watching us from that club over there, have you?"

Burgreen shook his head, surprised. "I'm not tailing either of you. Yet. Why?"

"Some fellow keeps staring at us," Henry said lightly.

"You didn't tell me, Henry." Emily was hurt. "What does he look like?"

"He looks like a small, well-groomed Poland-China pig. And we did tell you—Roscoe saw him—but you didn't even look up at the time."

Roscoe nodded. "That's right, Miss Murdock. He look and he look. I see him many time."

"He's probably unemployed," Emily decided. "You haven't found the gun?"

Burgreen said no, and he hadn't much hope of finding it. Emily wondered why the murderer wanted the gun back—if it was the murderer who took it from Roscoe. "If I killed somebody I'd just throw the gun away," she added.

Burgreen explained that all guns had numbers, and that if you had a permit to carry a gun, the number of your gun was on file in the police department.

"So you could trace this gun to the murderer?" she asked.

He nodded, gave her a quizzical smile, and stoked up his pipe with the Irish Mixture. "Suppose you had a gun you wanted to get rid of, Miss Murdock. What would you do with it?"

Emily tapped her front teeth with the handle of a paintbrush, a habit that made her look like a hungry gopher. "I'd go into the public library and stick it behind some old reference books."

"And when they dusted, which they probably do frequently, they'd find the gun, turn it over to us, and we'd trace it to you."

"No good? What about Link's shop window? He never cleans it out. You could hide a small elephant there for a month." She saw that he wasn't listening. "Why couldn't I just keep the gun myself? In my dresser drawer?"

Henry said if you were one of the suspects your apartment would be searched.

"But that's all been done now, hasn't it, Mr. Burgreen? Why couldn't the murderer take the gun home and keep it from now on?"

Burgreen lifted an amused eyebrow. "You've given me an idea, Miss Murdock. Of course it's an idea I had on Monday, but still—" His glance shifted to the windows and across the street. "Is that your man, Mr. Bryce?"

Henry looked. "No. That's Delaphine."

"So it is. Well, good-by, my friends." Burgreen was abruptly gone.

Henry wondered about Harmon's being in the club—James had frequently regretted the fact that Harmon didn't come round any more. Well, perhaps he had business with someone there. Perhaps he was nervous and wanted company. But a doctor ordinarily didn't have time in the middle of the afternoon to visit clubs.

Harmon had been looking down on the avenue. Now his eyes moved to the studio, he saw Henry, and waved. Henry waved back. Harmon turned and disappeared in the rosy interior, and Henry went on with his work. In a moment something caused him to raise his head again and he saw that the short, plump man was back at the glass, staring. Henry didn't know whether his expression was angry or wistful. Anyway, he didn't look happy.

Henry was about to turn back to his job when the little man took a small oblong package from his pocket and began picking at the string. He was evidently the sort of person who can't bear to cut string. He stopped working on the knot, felt the package with both hands. His face now was puzzled. He held the package close to the window, put on a pair of rimless spectacles, examined something on the wrapping paper. Henry could almost hear him say, "Oh," as if a question had been answered. He carefully adjusted the string, turned into the room, and disappeared.

"Henry," Emily pleaded, "the truckman's coming for those chairs. Are you ever going to finish up?"

Henry grunted, got back to work.

At a quarter past four a messenger arrived with another immense box from the Waldorf flower shop for Emily.

"Henry, I can't open it!" she cried.

"Try to hold yourself together," Henry suggested, deliberately cutting the green tape.

Emily yanked off the cover, gasped briefly at the armful of American beauties, and snatched the card. "Oh no!" she wailed. " 'To Miss Murdock, from a sincere friend.' This is driving me crazy, Henry. I don't have any sincere friends. Unless you count Link. Who could it be? You've got to find out before I lose my mind. Are you sure it isn't you? Roscoe, you wouldn't be so silly, would you?"

Roscoe shook his head, smiling. "I wish I could buy, but too much money, Miss Murdock."

Henry got the Waldorf florist on the phone. The clerk was courteous but uninformative.

"What did they say, Henry?" Emily demanded.

"They said the gentleman who ordered the roses for Miss Murdock does not wish his name disclosed. Very sorry, wish we could help you, and all that hogwash."

"It's a gentleman. That's something."

"They use that term indiscriminately on Park Avenue."

"Mr. Burgreen could find out, couldn't he? I'm going to ask him to, next time he comes."

They put the roses in the washbasin, and when the truckmen came for the chairs Emily gave each of them a rose. They obviously thought she was insane but were nice about it. Henry had taken off his apron and was washing up when he heard a female voice at the front of the shop. He came out, drying his hands on a towel.

Over the tops of various stacked articles of furniture he could see the cock feathers bouncing on a green velvet hat. "You are such a liar, Miss Murdock," the voice said evenly. "You had no more intention of delivering that bust than you had of jumping out the window."

Henry now recognized the short, compact figure of Mrs. Albert

Giddings, who reminded him vaguely of Lucille Watson. She turned on him. "And you, Mr. Murdock, you allow all this to go on without raising a finger. You're worse than she is because you at least have a mind. Your wife is an idiot, but you know what these things mean."

Emily was looking at Mrs. Giddings and smiling sweetly. She didn't say a word. She never did when they went on like that. She reached into her grimy smock pocket and pulled out a pack of mashed and twisted cigarettes, offered Mrs. Giddings one.

"No," cried Mrs. Giddings. "I don't want one of your filthy cigarettes. All I want from you is my bust."

"It's all ready," Henry said gravely. "Do you have your car? I'll take it down for you."

"No, really. You have learned all her tricks. The last time I was here—wasn't it during the Hoover administration—you were an honest man, Mr. Murdock."

Roscoe put a chair behind Mrs. Giddings, but she walked away from it. Henry went to the back of the studio, reached down the bust of Daniel Webster which was still wrapped, and brought it to the worktable. "You see, Mrs. Giddings, it's wrapped for delivery."

"I don't believe you. Unwrap it."

Henry cut the string, wondering uneasily if this really were the bust of Daniel—they hadn't looked at it since Roscoe brought it back. It was Daniel.

Mrs. Giddings looked it over suspiciously. "What's this lump on the back of the neck?"

"He had a mole," Henry said promptly. "We did a little research before we patched him up. Wanted to give you an authentic job."

"He hadn't a mole when I brought him in," Mrs. Giddings challenged.

"Oversight on the part of the sculptor," Henry answered. "I looked up Webster in Van Busckirk's *Peculiarities of American Physiognomy and Skeletal Aberrations*."

She looked straight through Henry, tapped the bust with her fingernail. "However, I'll take it as it is. I see no point in waiting another five years for you to remove this lump of plaster."

Emily beamed. "I knew you'd be pleased, Mrs. Giddings," she said. "Your hat is beautiful, and so becoming."

Mrs. Giddings ignored this, took a few strides about the studio, halted before a small table which bore an accumulation of dust and a couple of side chairs. "I might be able to use a table like this. What size is it?"

Emily took a yardstick from behind the radiator. "It's a very convenient little table," she agreed. "Handy for almost anything. We'd be glad to sell it to you."

While Emily measured it Mrs. Giddings tested the legs to see if they wobbled. "Not very good construction," she remarked. Emily said they would reinforce it for her, and pointed out that it was a very nice job of antiquing.

"I suppose you want some outrageous price for it?"

"Only forty-eight dollars." Emily beamed. "We made a very good deal on it ourselves."

Mrs. Giddings took the table and Roscoe carried it down for her, along with the bust of Daniel Webster.

"Aren't you ashamed, Emily?" Henry demanded, as soon as the door had closed.

"Not terribly."

"But you knew that was her table?"

Emily nodded. "You can't be too honest, Henry. It isn't practical."

"I wonder what made her come for that bust? After three years, why should she suddenly remember that she had a plaster at the Lentement studio?"

Emily shrugged. "Did you notice that she thought we were married?"

"Another thing," Henry went on, "she didn't ask us about the murder. Everybody else who comes in asks about Delaphine. They all seem to have heard about your luncheon date with her."

"Lots of people haven't heard about it," Emily said lightly. "Maybe Mrs. Giddings doesn't know we did work for Mrs. Delaphine."

Henry didn't pursue the subject. "Let's close up," he said. "I'm tired. And I'm not having dinner with you."

"You're not? But Henry—"

"Don't turn those pitiful blue eyes on me. I'm immune."

"Are you tired of me?"

"Very. Take your roses and go, like a good girl."

"Mr. Gottlieb will ask me if you're dead."

Emily sat at one of the round tables at the back of Gottlieb's Delicatessen and stirred her second cup of coffee. She hated having dinner alone. What was the matter with Henry now, she wondered.

Mr. Gottlieb came back and bent over her. "You no eat nothing, Miss Murdock. You sick?"

"No, Mr. Gottlieb."

"Where is Mr. Bryce? Why does he not come in tonight?"

Emily shrugged. "I don't know. He just said he didn't want to have dinner with me."

Mr. Gottlieb patted her shoulder. "Little fight, eh? Don't worry, he comes back tomorrow. Very nice fellah, Mr. Bryce. You should get married."

"I wish we would."

"He asks you?"

"No. I ask him practically every day."

Mr. Gottlieb shook his head. "Wrong. You make out you don' care about him. Make him jealous."

"How can I make him jealous? He doesn't even care when people send me two bushels of American Beauties. He thinks they have poor judgment."

Mr. Gottlieb smiled, patted her shoulder again. "I think about this for you," he promised. "Excuse me." He hurried to wait on a customer at the counter in front.

Emily thought of going to a movie, but the bill at Loew's was *Invisible Ray* and *Invisible Woman*, and she couldn't enjoy being frightened without Henry. Besides, she reasoned, you felt just as dismal in a theater as you did at home, and at home it didn't cost you anything.

She walked very slowly up Lexington Avenue, looking in each shop window, pausing a long time in front of Piecoli's Flower Shop to examine a flat bowl of camellias. She wondered where Henry was having his dinner. The disagreeable idea occurred to her that Henry might be out with some woman. She told herself that the woman must be over fifty, of a yellowish complexion, and very fat.

"You know she isn't, Emily," she said aloud. "Henry would pick some disgusting female with violet eyes and clean fingernails."

She turned and walked back to Sixty-second Street, climbed the stairs, and entered her own apartment. It was as difficult to cross as Broadway at lunchtime, but she wasn't going to do any cleaning and straightening tonight. She would take a hot shower and then get into bed and read.

Emily had accomplished the first two items when she discovered that she had left her glasses at the studio. She called Henry.

"I didn't think you'd be there," she said, surprised.

"Then why did you call me?"

"You sound all out of breath, Henry. I left my glasses at the studio. You don't mind running over for them, do you?"

Henry was very disagreeable. "I certainly do mind. You forget them at least three times a week, and it's time you learned. Go and get them yourself."

"But, Henry, I'm in my nightgown."

"Who cares what anybody wears on Lexington Avenue?"

"But it's cold out."

"Throw a blanket over yourself. Good-by."

Emily thought about this conversation for some minutes, sitting on the edge of the Pullman berth and twisting the chintz drapery. Henry must be very busy with something. She could try to go to sleep without reading but she knew it wouldn't work. Besides, she liked to see "What was justice in this case?" a page which the *News* ran daily for her special enjoyment.

After a while she tied a ribbon around her middle to hold up the nightgown, put on a coat and a pair of old pumps, and went down to the street. No one spoke to her as she walked quickly toward the studio.

She reached the entrance, pushed open the double doors at the foot of the stairway, and halted. One hand flew to her mouth. A man was sitting on the bottom step, gasping. His lips were purple. His hands clutched at his chest and his eyes seemed about to pop from their sockets.

"Can I help you?" Emily asked timidly, her own voice sounding strange.

The man tried to speak, made a funny choking noise, and collapsed in a small heap. Emily ran up the stairs to the studio door, scrambled in her pocketbook for the keys, got the door open, and stumbled through the yellow-and-crimson shadows thrown by the neon lights in the street. Her shaking hand knocked over a jar of paintbrushes as she reached for the light switch. She grasped the telephone, got the operator. "Give me the police," she whispered.

"What number are you calling, please?" inquired a calm mechanical voice.

"The police," Emily gasped.

"One moment, madam. I will give you the nearest precinct station."

The man down at Fifty-first Street asked what the trouble was.

"There's a man on the stairs," Emily told him. "I think he's dead. Please come right away."

"Could you give me the address, lady?"

Emily gave it, and added, "It's probably murder."

"What makes you think so? Never mind, we'll be up. Your name?"

"Emily Murdock."

"Stay there, Miss Murdock. We'll need you as a witness."

She replaced the phone, went back to the head of the stairs. The man hadn't moved. He must be dead, she thought. The police would come up and ask her a lot of questions. She looked down at herself. The nightgown was slipping to her ankles. She ought to go back to the washroom and get her smock and put it on.

It looked very dark at the back of the studio. There were so many large things—bookcases and screens and cabinets. There was the closed door into what had started to be a showroom and was now a storeroom.

"Don't be silly," she argued weakly. "Who would be up here?"

A door slammed at the back. She huddled tightly against the work-table. "It was the door to the washroom," she told herself. "It blew shut because the windows are open back there." But she couldn't move.

After a long time, in which she learned the outline of an empty Italian picture frame against the cracked plaster, a siren sounded down the avenue, came roaring nearer, stopped outside. Voices gathered. Emily gained courage, ran back to the washroom, seized the smock from the hook, returned to the front of the shop and was putting it on when heavy shoes came clumping up the stairs. She stuffed the nightgown into a vase, flung on her coat, and opened the door.

"Miss Murdock?" asked the officer.

Emily nodded.

"What do you know about that man down there?"

"Nothing."

"You never seen him before?"

"I don't think so. I didn't really take a very good look at him. He looked so awful."

"I see." The policeman went to the head of the stairs, called down to a companion, "Lady's up here, Joe. She don't know who he is. She says."

"What do you mean, 'she says?' " Emily demanded. "You ought to be glad I called you."

Joe came up, and Joe was Mr. McNulty.

"Why, hello," Emily said warmly.

McNulty was not cordial. "How come you're here at night?"

"I forgot my glasses, and I like to read in bed, so I came over here to get them."

He had to do some writing on a pad, and it appeared hard for him. "Reads in bed," he repeated. "Look here, Miss Murdock, you said over the phone the guy downstairs was murdered. How come you said that?"

"His lips were purple," Emily answered.

The other officer said maybe he had blueberry pie for dinner, and McNulty, pursing his lips, wrote again. "How did you know he was dead?" he persisted.

"He looked dead."

"For all you knew he was having a heart attack or the bends or something."

"But he looked dead," Emily pleaded.

The door opened and Henry came in.

"Henry!" Emily wailed. "They're giving me the third degree."

"Hello," he said calmly. "Find your glasses?"

"Henry, there's a dead man on the stairs."

"I know. I saw him."

"They're making me responsible for him."

"Now, lady," McNulty pleaded, "we gotta ask a certain amount of questions. You don't need to get sore. This your husband?"

"No," Henry put in emphatically. "Why all this battery of cops? Poor little guy probably just dropped dead of natural causes. No blood around."

"That ain't what the lady says when she calls up," the second officer told him.

At that moment Detective Burgreen arrived. "Who found this one?" he asked briefly.

"I did," Emily admitted. "I was just coming up for my glasses."

"Your glasses?" He gave her a frown.

"I like to read in bed. Is there anything wrong with that?"

"It's bad for your eyes," McNulty told her.

"I understand you told the precinct desk, Miss Murdock, that the man had been murdered. Just what gave you that idea—especially since the examiner hasn't found a thing to justify it?"

"His lips were purple," Emily said miserably. "Oh, Henry, make them stop, won't you? I'll never call the police again!"

Burgreen asked a few more questions, then he said they could go home. "You'll be here in the morning?" he added.

"Certainly," Henry promised, and taking Emily by the arm, led her down the stairs. There was a crowd around the doorway and they were loading the little man into the wagon from the morgue.

Mr. Gottlieb came toward them, his rosy face faded to a pale pink. "What is it?" he whispered hoarsely. "What happened?"

"Some fellow dropped dead on our stairs," Henry told him. "We'll be in for breakfast and tell you all about it." He pulled Emily on.

When they got to the corner and turned into Sixty-second Street he said, "Now for God's sake, Emily, let's hear what really happened."

"It's all your fault. You wouldn't go for my glasses, so I went there by myself and there was that poor little man at the bottom of the stairs— why did he have to die on our stairway? He wasn't quite dead when I found him, Henry, he was choking and gasping—it was simply horrible."

"You know who he was, don't you?"

Emily stopped short. "No. Do you?"

"If I'm not mistaken he's the same odd little fellow who kept watching us from the Thinkers' Club."

"Are you sure it's the same man?"

"I think so. Of course I may be wrong—I've never seen him close up before. But this fellow had the same round pink face and a bald pink scalp. Didn't notice if his glasses were lying around."

"I did. I stepped on them. Henry, don't you think it's a terrific coincidence for that particular little man to be dead on our stairs?"

Henry grunted, held open the door of her apartment building. "Not if he had a heart attack or something. He would naturally be walking in that neighborhood."

"I think you ought to tell Mr. Burgreen."

"He'll hear about it. If it's murder. And if it isn't murder it doesn't matter. Now go to bed and stop looking so old and wrinkled."

"You're so romantic, Henry. By the way—how did you happen to be out?"

"Came out for a pack of cigarettes."

"Oh. But you couldn't go over to the studio and get my glasses for me. Henry, I still don't have them!"

Henry grinned. "Typical. You can just get to sleep without reading tonight."

"I can't, with all this on my mind."

"Go to bed."

"Will you come up and look in the closets for me?"

Henry came, knowing it was the only way to settle Emily for the night. He was dog-tired and he wanted time to puzzle over what had happened.

"See?" he said triumphantly, opening the doors to both closets, moving the screen near the bathroom, and throwing aside the chintz draperies on the Pullman berth. "Nobody wants to rape Emily."

"I don't mind rape. It's murder."

"Good night." He patted her shoulder and left her.

Chapter 5

IF THERE was one thing Emily disliked more than getting up in the morning, Henry didn't know what it was. But when he walked into Gottlieb's at a quarter of nine there was Emily, chewing on a Danish pastry and optically devouring three newspapers.

"Henry," she cried, her mouth full, "they don't say a word about our murder!"

Henry sat down and Gottlieb came over. "A sad thing, that poor man last night," he said, dropping a gray look over his face for a moment and then, recovering his usual broad smile, he inquired what Henry would like for breakfast.

"Everything," Henry said briefly, and turned to Emily. "You mean there's no mention of his death?"

"You look. I don't see it."

Henry opened the *Tribune* to the death notices.

"Oh, way back there?" Emily frowned, stuffing another chunk of pastry into her mouth. "I thought that was just bankers and college presidents and other people we don't know."

"Here it is." Henry pointed to a short item at the bottom of a column. "Percy Ford, Jr. ... resident of the Thinkers' Club ... heart attack ... found last evening, etcetera, etcetera."

"It's our address," Emily admitted. "Then he was that same little man, and you were right, Henry. But he wasn't murdered."

"Don't be so downcast. People will think you get a commission on violent deaths."

"He could just as well have died in his club."

Gottlieb came up presently with scrambled eggs and ham and Henry asked him to bring Emily another pastry. He ate quickly, told Emily he had an errand and would be at the studio in a half-hour or so.

"You're getting awfully cagey, Henry," she protested. "Can't you tell me where you're going?"

He smiled and hurried out.

Henry had never entered the Thinkers' Club, and he was a little awed as he approached the desk and the thin-nosed gentleman behind it. There were daffodils in a glass vase at his elbow, and a woman in an apron was dusting the mail sections at his back.

"Good morning," Henry said, smiling. "I'm from the police department. I'd like to see Mr. Ford's room."

The clerk eyed him with a cold, glassy eye. Henry thought he was going to ask to see his card. Instead, he reached into a drawer, took out a cough drop, laid it on his tongue, and said, "Very well. Take the elevator. Third floor. Room 301."

"Key?" Henry asked.

"You won't need it." The man dismissed him by dropping his eyes to a basket of mail.

Henry took the elevator, walked along a corridor, turned a corner, saw an open door. It was marked 301. He stepped over the threshold.

"Good morning, friend," said Burgreen.

Henry flushed. "I was looking for you," he said quickly.

"Like hell you were. But you found me. What's up?"

"I had an idea. Maybe you have the same one. About Mr. Ford. It seemed just barely possible that he might not have died of a heart attack."

Burgreen smiled without humor. "What gives you this strange notion, Bryce?"

McNulty came out of the bathroom with an armful of bottles. "He sure took medicine, boss. Hello, Bryce. How's your wife?"

"She's not my wife," Henry said, but he didn't think the statement made any impression on McNulty, who was a man of implacable misconceptions. "I wouldn't have thought twice about Mr. Ford and his rather free use of our stairs if it hadn't been for his taking such an interest in the studio during the past few days. I told you there was a man who stared at our windows by the hour."

Burgreen nodded briefly. "McNulty, make a list of all these medicines and the names of the doctors. Seem to be several."

McNulty said yes, sir, but he looked troubled. Henry guessed that the application of pencil to paper was not one of McNulty's favorite pastimes. "I'll write 'em down if you read 'em to me, McNulty," he offered. "Providing, of course, the detective doesn't object."

Burgreen raised a black eyebrow, said "Hmm. Okay."

The list of medicines included an amazing number of digestive panaceas, some cough syrup, sleeping tablets of three varieties, and an empty pillbox marked "Digitalis," with directions for taking, and the name of the physician. Henry read it again. Dr. Harmon O. Delaphine. Several other prescriptions had Harmon's name on them, some for the stomach, some for the nerves.

Burgreen meanwhile had been sorting papers in a desk between the two large windows. The room, Henry noted, was spacious and exceptionally well furnished. The things appeared to be Mr. Ford's own, rather than club furniture. No imagination, but plenty of money.

Burgreen whistled, waved a paper. "Here's something that may interest you, Bryce."

Henry took the paper. It was a bill from the Waldorf-Astoria Florist for a dozen red roses to be delivered to Miss Emily Murdock. He didn't like it. He didn't like it at all. And yet he wasn't entirely surprised.

"That explains his watching the studio windows," he said. "He had a crush on Emily."

"But it doesn't explain why he was found dead on Emily's stairs, does it?"

"Those stairs lead up three flights," Henry objected. "They aren't our private stairs. And the little man had heart trouble. He was taking digitalis."

"We'll know more about that when we have the autopsy report. Another curious detail is the name of Dr. Delaphine on his medicines. It's almost too well tied up with a certain other recent death to be brushed lightly aside as accidental. Am I right?"

Henry said who was he to argue with an astute officer like Mr. Burgreen? The detective went back to his paper sorting and Henry idly picked up a bottle of B-complex capsules and unscrewed the tin cap. What good did it do a sedentary little man like Ford to take all these vitamins, he wondered. He shook out a few. They were shiny, almost black—dangerous-looking things to put in your stomach. His hand was damp and the capsules were fading onto his skin. They were fading purple.

"Burgreen," Henry said, "here's Emily's purple poison. Vitamin B."

"Sinister, these vitamins." Burgreen shoved away the letters he was reading. "Bryce," he said, too amiably, "tell me what you were doing last night. Where were you when Miss Murdock was finding the body?"

"At home, to a certain extent."

"To what extent?"

"I was jumping over the back fences between my apartment building and Mrs. Delaphine's house."

"Why?" Burgreen demanded.

Henry looked him in the eye. "There was someone going through her house last night."

"What? How do you know?"

"I saw a light from the street. It wasn't the kind of light a policeman would be using. Very small, very cautious. I thought maybe from the back I could get into the house and see who it was. I had an idea they might have come in that way themselves."

"Had they?" Burgreen asked.

"No. Back door padlocked."

"Any idea who was in there?"

"I couldn't get a decent view. All I saw was the flashlight—maybe one of these little key lights—going slowly from room to room. There were long periods when no light showed, and I thought the bastard had left the place, and then a light would show in a room on another floor."

"Could you tell whether it was a man or a woman?"

Henry shook his head. "I gave up and returned to my own building when no light appeared for forty minutes. It was a little cool squatting on the ground out there."

Burgreen sat back with a smug expression. "You realize what you've just told me, Bryce? Neither you nor Miss Murdock has an alibi of any kind for last night."

"Do we need alibis?"

"If Mr. Ford was helped out of this world, you certainly do."

"Doesn't make any difference that we didn't even know his name? Or maybe we like to kill people whether we know them or not. No hard feelings, just a little light recreation for long winter evenings."

Burgreen shrugged. "Maybe Lexington Avenue is more boring than the other avenues. I don't know. I live on the west side."

"Private phone?" Henry asked.

"Why?"

"We might want to reach you."

"No, I like my sleep and I like my Sundays. Now, if there's nothing further we can do for you, Mr. Bryce, perhaps you'd like to leave?"

Henry smiled. "I'm going. Would you mind not telling Miss Murdock who sent her those roses?"

"I won't tell her. Why should I?"

"Thanks," Henry said, and took the elevator down to the lounge. He stopped at the desk. "Mr. Burgreen will be up there a while longer," he said. "He would appreciate your sending him up a quart of milk and some soda crackers."

"Very well," said the clerk. His cool, distant expression became slightly marred with curiosity. "Find anything up there?"

Henry shook his head. "Can't say yet. Seems to have been a very quiet little fellow, doesn't he?"

"Yes indeed." The man leaned ever so slightly toward Henry. "But I don't think he wanted to be."

"No?" Henry lifted a casual eyebrow.

"There was a woman." The clerk looked Henry up and down to see what effect this stupendous announcement would have on his shape.

"Not really?" Henry said. "He didn't bring her here?"

"Not allowed to. But he could see her from here."

"You mean you know who the woman was?"

The man nodded proudly. "She works right across the street, in some sort of paint shop."

"How did you find that out?"

"Very easy. All his mail comes here. He got bills from the Waldorf flower shop recently. As nothing of this type had ever come for Mr. Ford, I was naturally interested."

"Naturally."

"So I held the envelopes against the lamp here—you can see through a great many letters that way."

"I'm sure you can. What sort of dame is she?"

"Oh, very pretty. I often noticed Mr. Ford looking across the street, so one day I stood behind him and saw what he was looking at. On my lunch hour I compared the address on the flower bills with that of this paint shop. They were of course the same. I wouldn't care for this lady myself, because she isn't really clean. But one must admit she has a pretty face and a very nice figure."

Saving his enjoyment of this description till later, Henry asked the man if Mr. Ford had had many friends at the club.

"Not many. He was alone a good deal. Dr. Delaphine was always friendly with him, of course, being one of his doctors. He was always going to a new doctor, to see if he couldn't find something new wrong with him. I think he did it for amusement."

"You say women aren't allowed here?"

"Oh, they may come in and wait a few minutes for their husbands here in the lounge. But they can't go into the smoking rooms or the bar. If they could, it wouldn't be a man's club, would it?"

Henry started to move away. The clerk leaned toward him, whispered, "There's something in the safe."

"Really?"

"Too bad for the lady that he dropped dead before he had an opportunity to give it to her." He blinked at Henry, waiting for the next question.

"What is it?" Henry asked obligingly.

"I'm not sure, but the package is small and heavy, and when you shake it, it makes a noise like jewelry."

Henry said that was very interesting. He thanked the man and walked over to the long windows facing Lexington Avenue, looked out as Mr. Ford had so often done. He could see Emily's sturdy hindquarters as she bent over to rub a chair rung with a rag. Roscoe was lackadaisically slapping paint. Emily looked up, apparently greeting someone, and then Henry saw Cornelia moving toward the windows. He'd better get over there.

Link hailed him as he passed the shop door. "Hey, Bryce, I want to see you about a murder."

"Be down again in a minute," Henry promised, and ran up the stairs to the studio.

"Where have you been?" Emily demanded. "You were working on a clue, weren't you?"

"Clue to what?" Cornelia asked.

"Aren't you up and about pretty early?" Henry looked at his sister. She had dark rings under her eyes and a pasty pallor, but then Cornelia never had been the outdoor type.

"Henry," Emily persisted, "where were you?"

Cornelia yawned. "I really think Emily ought to get married, she's so possessive. How would you like to meet a very rich man, Emily? He's interested in you already, so you wouldn't have to make an effort."

Emily looked at her suspiciously. "Who is he?"

"A friend of James." Cornelia sat down and crossed her fifty-one-gauge legs. "He's not young, but then neither are you."

"I'm as young as anybody else my age."

Henry thrust a pack of cigarettes at Cornelia. "You know Mrs. Albert Giddings, don't you?"

"Slightly. I haven't seen her in months. Why?"

"Mrs. Giddings came in yesterday for her bust of Daniel Webster and it just occurred to me that my sister might have reminded her of the existence of this plaster object."

"Why should I do that?" Cornelia refused his match and used her silver lighter.

"That's what I'd like to know." Henry met her long gray eyes, held them a moment, then they slid away to go darting over the shop.

"Look, you two, I want to know who this man is. Who wants to meet me, Cornelia?" Emily demanded.

"A moderately well-to-do gentleman. He lives at the Thinkers' Club."

"Not by any chance a Mr. Percy Ford?" Henry asked.

"Why, yes," Cornelia said, surprised.

"I'm afraid he's safely beyond Emily's reach. Didn't you hear about last night?"

Cornelia raised a doubtful eyebrow. "No."

"Don't you read the papers?" Emily asked. "He was in the *Tribune*. He died on our stairs last night." She waved in the general direction. "I found him."

Henry interrupted to say that the man had probably had a heart attack, stumbled through the doors, and died.

"How odd," Cornelia remarked, watching Emily spatter flyspecks on the chair. "He seemed in good health when I saw him."

"It was awful," Emily admitted, "and the police were very rude."

"Police—you called the police?"

"Naturally," Henry put in. "Who would you have called—the Great Neck Mother's Club?"

"Emily thought Mr. Ford had been murdered?"

"Emily loves violence. By the way, Cornelia, did you find anything in Cleo's house last night?" Henry asked casually.

"Was someone in her house last night?"

"You do have a key," Henry went on.

Emily interrupted. "What made you ask her that, Henry? Did you see somebody in Mrs. Delaphine's house, and if so, when? Is that why I had to get my own glasses and find a dead man?"

"To answer briefly and without evasion, yes."

"He didn't see the person's face," Cornelia said easily, lighting another cigarette.

"Maybe he did," Emily warned. "Henry is an awful liar when he wants to scare people. You don't scare easily, do you, Cornelia? I do. If I were you, a close friend of Cleo's, I'd be frightened."

"Silly," Cornelia said, not smiling. She went back to the washroom, leaving her bag on a chair. Henry picked it up and dumped the contents on the desk.

"That's dishonest," Emily protested.

He wasn't listening. At the top of the pile was an airmail letter from a Donald Clark, The Town House, Los Angeles. He opened it, flushed. "Uses pretty warm ink," he muttered.

"She's coming," Emily whispered fiercely. "Put the things back."

When Cornelia had gone, Emily asked, "Do you think she seemed nervous?"

"A little."

"Imagine that. Cornelia's always so sure of herself."

"Yes, that's why she jumps out of planes. I'm going down to see Link. Don't get into trouble while I'm gone."

"You just came in. You haven't done two licks of work this morning."

Henry went down to the street. He wanted to call Burgreen first, because the session with Link might be a long one. He found an empty booth in the drugstore, called the Thinkers' Club and then the precinct station, but Burgreen wasn't at either place. There was a number where he might be reached. Henry called it and got him at the morgue.

"I just found out," Henry began, "that Mr. Ford had asked my sister Cornelia to introduce him to Emily."

"That so? Found Mrs. Lord's phone number under his blotter."

"And even more interesting," Henry went on, "Cornelia has a letter in her handbag from a Mr. Donald Clark."

Burgreen went so far as to whistle. "Address?"

Henry gave it to him. "When you talk to her, please don't mention the roses, will you? Cornelia would love to tell Emily who sent them. Have they done an autopsy on the little man yet?"

"They're doing it. They have an observer in the person of Dr. Harmon Delaphine."

"That so? How does he get in on it?"

"As the subject's doctor he asked to be allowed to sit in, and they said okay." Burgreen hung up without saying good-by.

"He could have thanked me for my nickel," Henry muttered, and dropped on a stool at the counter. Ordinarily he took the coffee back to the studio in containers, but he wanted to think for a couple of minutes, and you couldn't think with Emily around.

Apparently Harmon Delaphine thought this autopsy was very important, or he wouldn't have taken a morning from his lucrative practice to attend. Henry wondered if Harmon still had a key to Mrs. Delaphine's house. If so, perhaps it had been Harmon who was there last night, going from room to room with a little flashlight. But what was he looking for?

Link came in, saw Henry. "Are you avoiding me, friend? We have a matter of importance to discuss."

"Emily's little dead man?"

"Nice way of putting it. Must have been pretty awful for her last night. Where were you?"

Henry said he had had various matters to attend to, such as watching Mrs. Delaphine's house.

"I thought the police attended to these things."

"They aren't watching it any more," Henry said. "Somebody was in there last night, looking for something. Must be something damned important, to take the risk."

Link ordered his coffee and a pastry. "Didn't have breakfast this morning," he said. "Too tired to get up in time. I'm giving up women."

"You're always giving up women."

"One at a time, yes. I mean all of them at once. You seem very cagey this morning, Henry. Who was the little guy they scraped off your stairs?"

"A Mr. Percy Ford, Jr. Thinkers' Club. Colorless, odorless, and tasteless."

"You don't think he was murdered, then?"

"Murdered?"

"Emily says he was murdered."

Henry watched Link take his first sip of coffee cautiously to see if it was too hot. He didn't know why he hadn't plunged right into the whole story, as he usually did with Link. Perhaps it was just the reluctant mood he was in. He had known Link for three years, and had always found him not only trustworthy, but kind and helpful and generous. A damned good friend. Why start having doubts now?

Link looked at him suddenly, grinned. "Now that you've got me in the electric chair—"

Henry felt himself turning red. "Maybe I've been taking myself too seriously," he admitted. "After all, I'm not the police department."

"Let's say you've been getting a great kick out of it," Link said easily. "And you're reluctant to let go a single suspect, including me."

"Right. There's something perverse in human beings that makes them secretly very happy when their best friends turn out to be rats."

Link nodded. "And don't forget that I'm a human being. I include you on my list of suspects. If you turned out to be Cleo's murderer, I'd probably buy myself a bottle of Peiper Heidsieck."

Henry told Link about the roses for Emily and the other things he had found out about Percy Ford Jr., and he also mentioned the fact that Dr. Delaphine was sitting in on the autopsy.

"Maybe he's just protecting himself professionally," Henry added. "In case the little man had taken an overdose of digitalis. Delaphine had prescribed digitalis for him."

"That right?" Link rubbed an eyebrow thoughtfully. "What is digitalis, exactly?"

"I don't know. Emily's going to be disappointed if it turns out he died of heart failure. She hopes he was shot with a poisoned arrow from the window of Gottlieb's Delicatessen." Henry looked at his watch. "She'll be down here with a hatchet if I don't get back. By the way, Link, who gets Cleo Delaphine's money, if any?"

"Didn't you know? Harmon. She left him everything, Cornelia says. Forgiving gal, wasn't she?" Link let this simmer in his mind a moment, then he said, "Cleo was still nuts about Harmon. I think she tried to call him when she was shot."

Henry put down the coffee. "You do?"

"Natural thing, wasn't it? He's a doctor, and he was the one person she really cared about."

It was a possibility, Henry admitted, but she couldn't have got through to Harmon or he would have called the police.

"Maybe she got through and Harmon is working a little blackmail." Link took a hearty bite of pastry. "That, of course, would be outside the code of the American Medical Association."

"And a little dangerous. Never blackmail a murderer, Link."

"I'll make a note of it," Link promised. "I don't think Harmon would blackmail anybody. He's a successful fellow, and rather proud of himself. Why upset things? I think, really, that Harmon did the killing."

"That of course wouldn't upset things." Henry asked the girl for another cup of coffee. "If Harmon did the killing then Mrs. Delaphine was not trying to telephone him."

"Why not?"

"She saw who did it."

"How do you know?"

"He was there," said a voice behind them.

Link and Henry looked up. Emily stood there in her smock and a short mink cape.

"What do you think of it?" she demanded. "Isn't it beautiful?"

"What?" Henry asked, looking her over.

"Link, do you like it? It's a tremendous bargain."

Henry groaned. "You're not falling for some furrier's line again, Emily?"

"It's not a line. This same cape, downtown in the stores, would sell for around a thousand dollars. He's letting me have it for eight hundred, because he has to raise the money."

"It's probably secondhand," Link suggested. "Who's selling it?"

"Cassamassima."

"That robber!" Henry cried.

"It's your fault." Emily told him, stroking the fur and looking very pleased with herself. "You were growling about his bill, so I called him up and asked him to pay the thirty-three dollars he owes us for painting his Venetian chest, and he said how about taking it out in trade? So I said all right, Joe. What have you got?"

"To collect thirty-three dollars you're going to spend eight hundred! Emily, I don't know what anybody can do with you."

"Seven hundred and sixty-seven," Emily corrected. "Isn't it beautiful? Don't I look wonderful?"

Henry looked her over, from her disheveled bronze hair to her paint-spattered suede pumps. "Venus rising from the ashcan. I think Link's right, the cape is secondhand."

"Sure it is," Link insisted. "Put your hand in the pocket and see if you don't find a piece of slightly used Kleenex."

Emily, crestfallen, slid onto a stool beside Link. "There's no kindness left in the world any more. All I ever get is criticism."

"Bring the lady a cup of coffee," Link told the counter boy.

"And besides," Emily went on bitterly, "you two were talking about the murders and leaving me out."

Henry pointed out that so far as anybody knew there had been only one murder, and he and Link hadn't been talking about anything Emily didn't know already.

"We were just saying Harmon must think it's important or he wouldn't take time to sit in on the autopsy," Link went on, being very open and friendly.

Emily looked at them sidewise, took a sip of the scalding coffee, and asked, "Who's having an autopsy?"

"I just found it out myself, Emily," Henry said defensively. "I called up Burgreen here in the drugstore."

"You couldn't possibly call him from the studio. Who's being cut open?"

"Your little friend of last night."

Emily said in that case someone else must think he was murdered, Mr. Burgreen, for instance. "I wish we knew a nice reporter who would call us up every hour or so and let us know the lowdown."

"Your friend Burgreen seems to do all right by Henry," Link remarked.

Emily frowned. "Yes, he does. I wonder why?"

"He wants the news to get around," Link suggested. "Henry's a talky sort of guy."

Henry was indignant. "I'm a silent philosopher."

The enormous bulk of Joe Cassamassima came through the swinging door from Lexington Avenue and his enormous voice opened fire. "Henry, my friend! Mr. Simpson, my friend. How are you? How's business? Myself I am going broke. You see this beautiful garment I am giving away to Miss Murdock?"

"We saw it," Link said, turning his back on Joe.

"It's a piece of perceptibly putrefying rabbit," Henry told him. "Take it away."

"My friend!" Mr. Cassamassima begged. "You do not know the history of this beautiful cape."

"I can guess. Somebody left it with you to cover the storage bill."

"Look! Is this a used garment? Obviously no. Is it worth two thousand cold cash? Obviously yes. I say this not as a merchant, not as a furrier who has been in the business forty-two years, but I say this as a friend, Mr. Bryce. Where can Miss Murdock get such a bargain?"

"Miss Murdock doesn't need such a bargain. Anyway, as a friend she wouldn't want to rob you of your profit. Take it away, Joe."

"Oh, Henry," Emily pleaded. "I like it."

"She likes it, Mr. Bryce. And for such a little price you would take away a lady's pleasure?"

"She doesn't need pleasure," Henry said. "She has me."

"It's secondhand," Link prompted. "It's secondhand, Joe, and you'd better be careful where you sell it."

Henry, who was leaning on his elbow and looking at Joe, thought he turned a little green at this remark. His sales talk flowed faster, became more pleading, there was even a faintly sobbing note in his voice. Somebody came briskly in from the street, and Joe turned hastily to see who it was. There was something fishy about the deal, Henry decided.

"What will you take for this stinking cape?" Henry asked abruptly. "Let's drop the oil and talk sense, Joe."

Cassamassima glowed with new hope. "Seven hundred," he whispered.

"Nuts." Henry turned away, finished his coffee.

"Six hundred and fifty?" Joe asked.

Emily looked from one to the other with her mouth open.

"It's secondhand," Link repeated, helping Henry.

"I think it's worse than that," Henry grunted. "I never thought Joe would stoop to stolen goods."

Joe stepped close to his ear. "Mr. Bryce," he whispered, "please! You ruin me. You make lies about me. How about four hundred and fifty?"

"Stay with it and he'll give you a bonus for taking it, Henry," Link suggested. "I think maybe you've got something. Joe, are you a fence?"

"A fence? What is that, a fence?" Cassamassima turned to Emily, who looked dazed. "Miss Murdock, you know me for many years. Many, many, many years. Am I a crook? Yes or no?"

"Yes, I guess so," Emily said kindly. "But you're a nice man, Mr. Cassamassima. You couldn't help it if the dye came off the muskrat coat."

"Yes, what about that muskrat coat you sold Emily way below cost?" Link inquired. "The cape is secondhand, Joe."

Joe turned his back on the two men. "Miss Murdock," he said in a low, confidential voice, "you have sense. Don't listen to them. They don't want you to have this cape because they hate to spend money. Men don't like to spend money. But you can have it. I make a price you can pay without them. You are a businesswoman. You see a bargain. Three hundred dollars."

"I'll take it," Emily said promptly, opening her green kid bag. "Is a check all right?"

Joe shook his head. He needed cash.

"Henry, lend me ten dollars for a deposit, will you?"

"I will not. I disapprove of the whole transaction."

Link took out his wallet and gave Emily the ten dollars. "Of course you may go to jail," he warned.

"I don't care." Emily pulled the cape about her. "It's worth it."

Joe said he had to have the rest of the money within an hour. Emily left them to go to her bank, and Joe hurried out with her, not anxious to engage in further conversation with Henry and Link.

"I wish you hadn't given her the ten dollars," Henry said.

"The thing is worth a lot more than three hundred," Link protested. "And Emily wanted it."

"If it's worth a lot more, why is Joe selling it cheap? There's something wrong with the deal, Link."

"Sure. It may prove interesting to have the cape."

"It wouldn't be interesting if they arrested Emily for having it. You notice he wouldn't take a check. And I'll bet he won't give her a bill of sale."

"Oh, well." Link shrugged. "A lot of stolen furs get sold around town and nobody is the wiser. Funny, though. I didn't think Joe was quite that low, did you?"

"No. I knew he was a pirate, but I assumed it was legitimate preying on the vanity of women."

"I've got to get back to the shop." Link stood up.

Henry sat there alone for a while. They had a great deal of work to get out, but he didn't feel like striping chairs. After a couple of cigarettes he called the Seventeenth Precinct and asked for Burgreen. The detective wasn't in. He asked for McNulty. Somebody called him away from his solitaire and he came on, very brisk.

"This is Bryce, Mr. McNulty. Do you have an autopsy report on Percy Ford, Jr.?"

It took McNulty a while to work his way around the problem. "What do you want to know?" he inquired, when this had been illuminated in his mind.

"I wondered if you knew yet whether he died a natural death? My partner, Miss Murdock, is pretty upset about the little fellow, since she found him, and I've been hoping it would prove to be a heart attack or something like that, just to relieve her mind."

"We don't give out that information, Mr. Bryce."

"But a police officer is supposed to keep the peace, isn't he? As long as Miss Murdock thinks this man was murdered there'll be no peace on Lexington Avenue."

McNulty thought about that. "You can ask the sergeant. I don't know."

"Never mind." Henry hung up. He dialed Harmon Delaphine's apartment number. Harmon wasn't there. He wasn't in his office, either.

When Henry got back to the studio Emily was standing before a long gilt mirror looking at herself in the mink cape.

"Did you pay Joe?" Henry asked.

"Of course. I'm dying to have Hilda see it. She'll turn green. I called her and told her to come over as soon as she gets rid of her customer."

"In that case I'll go out for lunch."

"Henry, you haven't done a thing this morning. Oh, hello, Hilda."

Hilda Leghorn came in, looked at Henry as if he were a flyspeck on a plate. "I hear you found a body."

"Emily found him," Henry corrected.

"Why didn't you tell me?" Hilda regarded Emily with an aggrieved frown.

"Oh, that—that's old stuff now, Hilda. Look." Emily walked up and down displaying the cape.

"What did you do when you found the body?"

"I called the police."

"Oh no!" Hilda clasped her hands to her artificial bosom. "Never do that!"

"Why not?" Emily demanded.

"The person who finds the body is always stuck with the murder. You'll never get out of this, Emily," she added cheerfully.

Henry said that was nonsense, nobody thought Emily had killed the little man, in fact it was extremely likely he had died a natural death, as he had a bad heart.

"There," Emily said, smiling, "you see it's really nothing. Now look at my cape!"

"Oh, you've had your old muskrat made over."

Emily went on smiling. Emily always went on smiling. "It's mink and you know it. Cassamassima let me have it for practically nothing."

Hilda negligently felt a corner of the cape. "It is mink. I don't know why anybody wants mink. All the Park Avenue whores have mink. I wouldn't be seen in it myself."

Henry turned away and began vigorously putting stripes on Mr. Di Nobili's chair.

Emily didn't say a word. Emily never really believed she had been kicked in the teeth until you picked up one or two and showed them to her. He could see her face in the mirror and it was crestfallen.

"Link thought it was pretty, anyway," she said mildly.

"Link doesn't know one fur from another. And he always says what you want him to say, Emily. He's nuts about you, God knows why. How much did you pay for this thing?"

"I don't think I'll tell you." Emily took the cape off and folded it inside out and put it on the top shelf of a cabinet.

"There's something familiar about it," Hilda said suddenly, taking the fur down again and holding it at arm's length. "Emily, it's secondhand.

That's very dangerous, you know. You haven't any idea who may have worn this cape, maybe they had some dreadful disease—syphilis or something."

"Oh, Hilda!" Emily shuddered. "Henry, do you think they had a disease?"

"Sure," Henry grunted. He looked out the window. "There goes a customer into your place, Hilda."

"You just want to get rid of me. I'm positive I've seen this cape before, Emily." She threw it back on the shelf. "Well, so long, dear. I hope you won't regret putting all that money into something you'll hardly ever wear."

Henry waited until he heard the downstairs door close. "The bitch," he said solemnly.

"I feel awful," Emily confessed. "And I was so proud of it."

"Look, Emily." Henry put down the striping brush and took both her hands. "It's a beautiful cape and it looks wonderful on you and it was a great bargain. Now, do you feel better?"

"No." Emily blew her nose. "Because you don't mean it."

"I do mean it. I love mink. I adore mink on you. I think you should have had a mink coat years ago. I think you should have a mink dog to go with it. There."

"Henry, you're sweet." She regarded him thoughtfully. "Would you like to pay for it?"

"And why the hell you put up with that slut from across the street is beyond me."

"But she's my best friend, Henry. She saved my life when I thought I had appendicitis."

"How?"

"She found out I didn't have it." Emily began to worry in another direction. "Do you think Hilda really has seen the cape on somebody else?"

"They're all alike. How would she know one from another?"

This one, Emily pointed out, was scalloped around the bottom. Henry said so were a thousand others.

Late in the afternoon Burgreen came in. Henry suspected that the studio held a reluctant fascination for the detective. He could have phoned, but he had taken the trouble to come.

"You have nothing to worry about, Miss Murdock," he said at once.

"Autopsy on Ford showed nothing toxic. Cardiac failure."

"What's that?" Emily asked.

"His heart stopped beating."

"Why?"

"We don't know."

"You see—he was poisoned."

"But, Miss Murdock," Burgreen persisted, smiling patiently, "there was no evidence of poisoning."

"His lips were purple."

"That was simply a dye in the gelatin capsules he was taking. Bryce could have told you that. If it makes you feel any better, his stomach was also purple."

"Then why did he die?"

Burgreen threw up his hands. "I'll leave her to you, Bryce. You must be accustomed to this sort of thing." He buttoned his overcoat and departed.

"He's wonderful," Emily sighed. "Do you think he's telling the truth?"

"Of course."

"How disappointing." She gazed wistfully across at the Thinkers' Club. "I thought it was going to turn out to be something really gruesome. Imagine dying of a purple stomach."

Chapter 6

AT HALF-PAST SIX that evening Henry, having arranged with Link to take Emily to dinner, climbed the steps between the stone lions, crossed the wide terrace where in warmer weather people discussed the state of the world, climbed the second flight of steps protected for winter by a supplementary covering of wooden stairs with railings, and entered the public library.

It was a cold night and they weren't letting in any outside air. The atmosphere of research was a little thick, but since it was free you couldn't complain. He entered an elevator cage which rose halting and jerking to the third floor. He walked down a corridor hung with prints of early New York and found himself in the center of a vast room entirely lined with card boxes. It was a long time since Henry had had to use a book and he felt self-conscious. He hoped nobody would notice as he made his way around, looking for the d-i's. He found the box, took it to a table, and under the watchful eye of a young lady in a blue raincoat who had apparently forgotten why she was there, he fingered his way to digitalis. It was a well-covered subject.

Now that he had found it, he didn't know which book to ask for. What, exactly, did he hope to discover, anyway? His eyes opened wider as he read: "See poisons." He hadn't known it was poisonous. There was a work entitled: *The Standardization of Digitalis*: A comparative study of some of the methods of assaying digitalis, with a description of an improved modification of the one-hour frog method, by Maurice Isadore Smith and Wm. T. McClosky.

That didn't seem to be quite what he was looking for. Better try poisons. He replaced the box, as the notices requested, and began a search for the p-o's. The box was down. He sidled behind several people at tables, reading the letters on their boxes, and found the one he wanted in the hands of a trim white-haired gentleman in spats and pince-nez. He was taking his time.

Henry stood on one foot and then the other, occasionally letting out a sigh.

The gentleman turned round. "Haven't you something to do, young man?"

Henry smiled affably and continued to stand. The fellow seemed to be working on poisons too. Prosperous, plump, a little flushed, as if he ate too well. Certainly not thinking of ending his own life. Maybe his wife was annoying him. Or an extra mistress.

"Really," he said, turning round again, "I'd appreciate your going away."

"Thinking of poisoning someone?" Henry asked sociably.

The man glared. "Bureaucracy," he growled, jamming the pencil into his vest. As it was chained to the table it snapped out as he walked away.

Henry applied himself to the cards, reflecting that probably some lady had him to thank for a slight extension of her days. He found what sounded like a reasonably nontechnical toxicology by a professor from Princeton and a sergeant of the New Jersey State Police. It was on the shelves in the reading room, and an attendant gave it to him without asking any personal questions. The library didn't seem to care whether people poisoned each other or not.

He sat down happily with his prize and found out immediately that digitalis was "foxglove, purple foxglove, or fairy gloves." Nice to die of fairy gloves. Something called digitoxin came from the same plant, and one tenth of a grain of that might kill a man in a few hours. "Most active and toxic glucoside of the *Digitalis purpurea*."

He was conscious of noisy conversation at the end of the room—people without proper respect for the silent halls of learning.

"Henry!" Emily cried. She hurried toward him, followed by Link. "He has it, Link," she said, pouncing on the book. "Henry's reading up on digitalis."

"Quiet," Henry begged. "Sit down."

They sat on either side of him.

Emily was of course wearing the cape, and she flipped it over the back of the heavy oak armchair. "You think Mr. Ford was murdered, don't you, Henry?"

"People are listening," Henry pleaded.

Link had taken the book and was reading the few short paragraphs. Henry pointed out the digitoxin factor. Link read on, frowning. "Look at these tests for identification, Henry. They could tell right away if he had taken digitoxin. So that's out."

Henry agreed. "But look at the difference in the normal doses for various types of digitalin. For instance, you take two grains of U.S.P. XI and a thirtieth of a grain of Digitalinum Verum."

Emily said he was getting the book dirty, pointing. "What are you proving, anyway?" she said.

"Please shut up. We'll speak to you when we get outside," Henry said. He and Link made some notes and then gathered Emily and left the building.

At the top of the steps Emily paused. "I'd like to scream a little if you don't mind. It was so quiet in there."

"Go ahead."

She screamed. The sound was almost inaudible against the traffic noise from Fifth Avenue.

"New York is an ideal place for a murder," Link observed. "Now suppose Henry and I were to knock you off right here, Emily. Nobody would know. Nobody would hear you scream, because you do it so feebly. They wouldn't accuse us, because we're supposed to like you. You'd be another unsolved crime for the *Mirror*. 'Beautiful paint slopper strangled on library steps. Police baffled. Library authorities give no clue. Lions indifferent.' "

"I wish somebody would give a party," Emily said suddenly as they went down the steps. "A party for all the suspects."

"Why don't you?" Henry suggested. "You're a woman of some means now. Mink coat."

"Maybe I will."

Henry was sorry he had made this flippant suggestion, because when Emily gave a party Henry did the work.

Link returned to digitalis. "Suppose I were taking one kind of digitalis and you were taking another, and the doses were entirely different. I could give you one of my pills, secretly, of course, and then when you got around to that particular pill you'd drop off."

"But I should think everybody would be taking normal doses no matter what particular preparation they were using. Wouldn't a pill be a normal dose?" Henry objected.

Link thought that over. "You'd have to make a special pill, maybe. Could you make a pill, Henry?"

"I could, yes. I was once a pharmacist's assistant."

"Could anybody?"

"I don't think so. Anyway, you can't buy poisons without a prescription."

Emily asked why you couldn't grow some foxglove in a window box, with chives and petunias.

"If anybody did that, then they planned a long time ago to murder Mr. Ford. And there must be a reason way, way back," Henry added.

"I don't see why you both go on and on about an overdose of digitalis," Emily protested, "when Mr. Burgreen told you the man died of heart failure. He'd have told you if there was an extra amount of the medicine in the man's stomach, wouldn't he?"

"Would he?" Henry asked.

"He has an honest face," Emily reminded him.

Link thought Mr. Burgreen would tell them anything he considered expedient. "But according to our reasoning, Henry," he added, "no ordinary citizen could have given Mr. Ford a fortified dose of his own medicine. It would take a doctor to do it—in short, Harmon Delaphine."

"But, Link," Emily protested, "you have to be intimate with somebody before you want to kill them. Harmon was only Mr. Ford's doctor."

Link laughed. "That depends on your motive, Emily. In robbery you don't have to be friendly."

"This wasn't robbery. Could we have something to eat?"

"Again?" Henry groaned.

Link said it was a reflection on his qualities as a host, but they both knew that she ate merely for recreation and that it had nothing to do with the actual needs of the organism.

They walked up Fifth Avenue, arguing amiably about where they would go to restoke Emily. It had begun to rain, and the red lights took on violet tones dipped in the blue of the wet pavement.

"Beautiful on a rainy night, isn't it?" Henry murmured, looking far up the Avenue.

"Umm. I think I'd like steamed clams," Emily decided.

It was toward the bottom of the plate of clams that Emily came up with her idea. They were sitting in the dim pinkish light of a small French restaurant, comfortably supplied with a bottle of sauterne, baskets of crusty bread, and large cups of chicory coffee with hot milk. Emily had insisted that they order something unusual. Henry refused, saying he had long since ceased to explore the world with his stomach. Link, to please her, had ordered a fried skate and immediately decided that it was a laboratory not a gustatory item.

He was poking holes in its hide with his fork when Emily said, "I think you're both awfully stupid."

"New evidence, or just a summary of past experience?" Link inquired.

"If a person is taking digitalis, he needs digitalis, doesn't he?"

They nodded, waiting.

"He'll die without it?"

They nodded again.

"Put some pills in his pillbox that don't have anything in them at all—maybe just some cornstarch and aspirin or something."

Henry put down his fork. "Emily, that's very good."

"Thank you."

"She's got something," Link agreed. "Get hold of a common pill—aspirin, quinine, a bicarbonate preparation—that looks like the tablet Mr. Ford has been taking. He thinks he's getting his medicine, and he isn't at all."

"Maybe he took capsules," Emily suggested.

"You can get quinine in capsules. Other stuff too." Link trimmed the leather binding off the skate and wound it around his fork reflectively. "All this is very interesting but purely academic. There's no evidence whatever that anybody had a reason to kill Mr. Ford. Emily is looking for excitement."

"How about you?" she demanded. "It was your idea to go to the library. And how about Henry? I didn't invite him there." Link gave her an odd look, seemed about to reply, turned instead to Henry. "Did you ever hear what became of the bird cage you were taking to the Belasco Theatre that night?" he asked.

"No. Probably it's been reduced to an ounce of potash or something in the city garbage distilleries. Still, it might turn up, you know. Sometimes a junk man picks a thing like that out of a trash can and sells it and eventually it works its way back into the decorating market. On the other hand, it might be purchased down on Canal Street by a nice old lady who keeps birds."

Emily hadn't thought about the bird cage until now. She wanted to take a taxi to Canal Street instantly and look for it. Henry explained with patience that it might be anywhere from Montauk to Jersey City and that he had merely mentioned Canal Street as an illustration.

"What good is an illustration if it isn't the truth?" she argued. "You said it was on Canal Street."

"I didn't say it was on Canal Street. Now forget about the cage, will you?"

"I didn't bring it up. Link mentioned it first. What made you think of it, Link?"

"I don't know. Just struck my fancy. Maybe the murderer left a thumb in it or something."

"The murderer?" Emily looked startled.

"The murderer is usually the man looking for the gun," Henry grunted. "The man who slugged me and thought he was getting the bust of Daniel Webster wanted the gun in the bust. See?"

"I'm not sure." She went on eating clams in a stolid way, and when she had quite finished she announced that she wanted to go and see Harmon Delaphine.

Henry said it was much too late. Link wanted to know what excuse they could give for calling on him.

"We're friends," Emily said. "We don't need an excuse. He can tell us what happened at the cutting up of Mr. Ford."

"If he wants to," Henry added.

"Finish your coffee, Link." Emily took out her compact and pounded powder into her skin.

"It was so comfortable here." Link sighed.

"Women hate to see men comfortable. I'll pay for this." Henry took out his wallet. "We're walking to Delaphine's."

"It's too cold and rainy," Emily protested.

"Ladies in mink never get cold."

They walked, bucking the wind across town, Emily complaining every step of the way—her feet hurt, she was cold, she was getting indigestion from hurrying. Nobody listened to her.

Harmon's apartment, on Park Avenue near Sixty-eighth Street, had the usual admiral at the door, and when Henry asked for Dr. Delaphine he said, "Yes, sir, four-ten."

"Shall we go up?" Emily hesitated.

"Whose idea was this?" Henry demanded, stopping in the center of the long Chinese carpet.

"I know, but I feel kind of silly, now that I'm here. We don't really know Harmon well enough to come barging in. Suppose he has a lady with him?"

Link and Henry shoved her into the elevator and in a moment they were standing in front of the blue door of number four-ten.

"It needs redecorating." Emily chipped off a bit of paint with a fingernail. "Wouldn't you think they'd be more careful on Park Avenue?"

The door opened, cutting off her remarks. Harmon peered at them, blinked nervously, took off his spectacles. "Oh, hello," he said, smiling. "Come in. I don't see very well—forgive me."

"Hope you aren't busy. Emily wanted to ask you about something," Henry explained.

Harmon ushered them through the foyer, settled them in comfortable chairs, and said dryly, "And you always do what Emily wants, of course."

"It's easier than being torn limb from limb," Link told him. "Very effective, that rhododendron leaf, Delaphine."

"It is, isn't it?" Emily agreed. "You can't have a room today without some kind of dendron, philo or rhodo or something. What a pretty little box, Harmon." Emily picked it up, opened it, smelled it, took a cigarette from it. "Even if it is an imitation." She got up again, walked around the room.

"You can take the cape off now," Henry said. "Harmon has seen it and he isn't going to say a word."

"The cape?" Harmon repeated. His weak blue eyes seemed to come forward in his face. "Why, it's a very lovely one, Emily. I should have noticed it at once." His gaze traveled over it repeatedly. "Shall I hang it up for you, my dear? It's rather warm in here."

"Oh no, thank you. I like to wear it." Emily sat down. "What we really came to see you about," she went on quickly, "was cutting up Mr. Ford this morning. I think he was murdered, don't you?"

Harmon smiled faintly, went back to his chair. "No, Emily."

Emily looked at Link and Henry, but they let her flounder. "We've thought of a way he could have been murdered that would be perfectly safe for the murderer. And he wouldn't have to be a doctor to do it, either, Harmon, so that makes things look better for you, doesn't it?"

Delaphine raised his limp hands helplessly. "Am I under suspicion?"

"Everybody is, naturally," Emily told him. "At first we thought it would have to be a doctor, because none of us except Henry knows how to roll a pill. You could easily have made up a batch of pills for Mr. Ford, with lovely overdoses of digitalis, but we couldn't, and Cornelia couldn't."

Delaphine smiled at Henry. "Emily suspects your sister of murder?"

"Of course."

"I don't quite follow your reasoning, Emily," the doctor went on, "since Mr. Ford had not taken an overdose."

"That's where our brilliant discovery comes in," she said. "Why couldn't you kill Mr. Ford with an underdose? No dose at all?"

Link explained this, and Delaphine found it interesting but improbable. "Since the police do not believe the man was murdered, I can't see why you three are convinced of it."

"Two murders are always better than one," Emily pointed out. "And Cleo's was so terribly obvious. This is much more brainy."

"But the man had no enemies—I knew him fairly well, used to see him and talk with him often at the club. He was a comfortable, harmless bachelor."

"Those are the people who get killed—they accidentally find out something and the murderer has to kill them."

Delaphine shook his head. "A wise murderer isn't going to scatter two sets of clues. Wouldn't you all like a drink?" Without waiting for an answer he went into his service pantry and began rattling ice cubes and glasses. It was a nice, promising sound, Henry thought, leaning back in his chair and glancing round the room.

Emily tiptoed over to him. "We mustn't drink anything," she whispered. "Let's get out of here."

"Why?"

"I'll tell you later." She went to the pantry. "Harmon, we must go, really. Don't bother with drinks."

Link protested. "We've just come, Emily. And the whole thing was your idea."

Harmon stood in the doorway, a bottle in his hand. "Surely you have time for a short one?"

"No, we really must go. Come on, Henry." She was already in the foyer.

Harmon grinned. "I believe she thinks I'm going to poison the lot of you."

"Oh no," Emily said quickly. "We just happen to have an engagement."

"We haven't any engagement," Link contradicted. "I'm in favor of the drink." He settled back on his spine and helped himself to one of the doctor's cigarettes.

"I'll open a fresh bottle—in fact, I'll let you open it yourself, Emily," Harmon offered, humoring her.

She hesitated, enlarging the hole in her glove with a fingernail. "I don't like to be rude, Harmon. It's just that I'm not quite ready to die."

The three men laughed, and Emily, flushing, went into the pantry and mixed the drinks herself with tap water, apparently convinced that Harmon could not have contaminated the entire city water supply.

When everyone had a glass Harmon needled Emily in a good-humored way. "You wouldn't care to tell me why you developed this sudden devastating suspicion?"

"I can't."

"Too bad." He shook his head. "I was counting on you to help me cover up this obvious error before Mr. Burgreen discovered it."

Emily removed the cape and threw it over the arm of her chair. The gesture shattered Delaphine's composure. He stared at the wrap, almost feeling it with his eyes.

"I'm glad," he observed in a slightly husky voice, "that the decorating business is so good these days, Emily."

"Oh, it was a terrific bargain, Harmon. Otherwise I could never have got it. Cassamassima practically gave it to me. Henry says it was stolen."

"What would you say, Delaphine, if someone offered you that litter of animals for three hundred dollars?" Henry demanded.

Delaphine raised a twitching eyebrow. "Seems a little low, doesn't it? However, the fur market is very poor."

They stayed a polite five minutes after their drinks were gone. Down in the street, and out of earshot of the doorman, Henry demanded, "Now will you please explain that ridiculous scene, Emily?"

Emily opened her cape, took from under her left arm a small painted box. "Remember that?"

"Emily, you stole that from Harmon's apartment."

"Certainly. And we made it for Mrs. Delaphine."

"What if we did? I don't remember it."

Link was interested. He took the box and examined it under a street light.

"It has a secret compartment. And do you know where Harmon got it?"

Henry said he supposed Harmon had got it from his wife.

"That is not the point. He got it from her after he killed her, Henry."

Link asked what she meant.

"The box was in Mrs. Delaphine's apartment when I went there that night to get my ring—the night she was killed. I know it was there, because I said something to her about it—you know, chitchat. 'We did that.' 'Oh yes, I believe you did, Miss Murdock,' and all that crap."

"Emily, no lady uses that word."

Emily took the box from Link, pressed a spring, and a tiny drawer popped out. "It's empty!" she cried.

"What did you think would be in it?" Link inquired.

"I don't know. I suppose he took it out."

Henry was thinking. "You're positive this box was in Mrs. Delaphine's house when you went there to get your ring? Sure it wasn't the day you did the work for her?"

"Henry, I know when I see things."

"Sometimes I wonder. But assuming you're right, Harmon could have taken the box without killing his ex-wife."

"But he didn't say he was in her house that night, Henry."

"That's it—if he didn't kill her, why not admit he was there?" Link agreed.

Henry said that would increase Burgreen's suspicions. Harmon was a likely suspect in any case, and to admit his presence on the scene would be damaging. "Know what I think? Harmon is the fellow who went through her house last night. He was looking for something which might be in this box, so he took the box away with him."

Emily said, "Why not open the drawer and take what he wanted and leave the box in the house?"

"He may have forgotten how it opened. Perhaps he never knew— Cleo had it made for her own use, you know. He didn't want to spend much time there fooling with it, so he took it home."

Link wondered how Harmon could have gotten into the house, and they decided he probably still had keys. "Did you notice how he looked at Emily's cape?" he added. "Either he's seen it before or he thinks he has."

"Oh dear!" Emily said, alarmed. "Maybe the cape's mixed up in the murder."

"Did you examine it for bloodstains?" Link asked.

"Stop it. I'll throw it away."

"Do you know Emily Murdock? She's the decorator who wears bloody mink."

Emily showed up at Gottlieb's in the morning, with the cape.

"Henry," she said, "I'm not sure I'm going to like having a coat you've got to wear every day, or put in a safe."

Henry took a moment from the *Tribune* to point out that since it cost only about as much as Persian paw or sable-dyed muskrat she needn't be so careful of it.

"If somebody gave me a diamond," she countered, "would I drop it in the gutter because it didn't cost me anything? When are you going to, Henry?"

"Going to what?" He turned around and called to Gottlieb for more coffee.

"You'd better get over to the studio," Emily prodded. "I'm going to have my hair done."

"Is that so? What's the occasion?"

"The party."

Henry wanted to know what party, and Emily reminded him that she was giving one for the suspects.

"You haven't even asked the people."

"I feel better asking them with my hair done. Then I know I'm all prepared. I'll have it tomorrow, before the idea gets stale."

"Henry, of course, will do the unimportant chores like buying the liquor and the food."

"Oh, you will?"

Henry sighed, and Emily looked at him anxiously. "You look sad, Henry."

"I feel sad."

"Why?"

"Does there have to be a reason?"

"Nobody feels sad without a reason. Either you've lost your wallet with over a dollar in it, or you're thinking about the future of man, or somebody you like told you you were getting fat, or your stomach is upset."

Henry shrugged. "None of these interesting items applies to my case. I just feel sad, that's all."

"You can't. It isn't natural." Emily leaned toward him, examining his face. "Your color is good. You must have a secret worry that even you don't know about."

"I have."

"Henry, you didn't kill Mrs. Delaphine and Mr. Ford, did you?"

"My secret worry is sitting across from me now, gazing down my throat like a vulture looking for signs of fatal disease."

"A shapely vulture, or just an average-run vulture?" She gave him a sudden hopeful smile. "Henry, you don't mean you're weakening?"

Henry swallowed his coffee and went over to the studio, leaving Emily to enjoy a couple of hours of red-hot gossip in Hilda Leghorn's beauty shop. He was putting dust on an eighteenth-century desk when Emily came tearing up the stairs.

"Henry!" she gasped. "The bird cage—someone's got it—they told Hilda about it—she doesn't know it's ours, but from what she said I know it's the one!"

"Really?" Henry went on with the dust.

"Well, aren't you going to do something?"

"What do you want me to do?"

"Go and get it—or look at it anyway. You said it might have a clue. You and Link both said so."

Henry asked if she knew who had the cage. He felt very skeptical about its being the same. Hilda had obtained all the details. The customer had bought the cage from a pushcart in Canal Street while looking for silverware down there. It was in almost perfect condition, and a tremendous bargain.

"And how do you propose to get it back?" he inquired.

"You always have ideas for these things, Henry. Just say we need it. Mrs. Cormorant would be pleased if we could send it to her, wouldn't she? I've already asked Hilda to the party, I hope you don't mind."

"You've insured a delightful evening."

"Now, Henry. You don't like her because she's a hairdresser."

"I wouldn't like Hilda if she had a half interest in the Elysian Fields."

"That's silly—she doesn't know a thing about farming. Anyway, she's bringing a quart of coleslaw. You can't say she's stingy." Emily went back to the washroom and climbed into the denim pants she was wearing with a pink smock that week.

"Where's my nice thin brush?" she complained, moving the paint cans on the worktable and throwing accusing glances at Roscoe and Henry.

Roscoe found it for her. Roscoe liked interruptions. He paused to look down into the street. "Mr. Lord is coming over. He has a paper bag."

"I hope it's cheesecake," Emily said, drooling.

It was shrimp chips. "Maybe I ought to have brought beer with them," James apologized. "It did seem a little cold for beer."

"Guess what?" Emily demanded, wiping her hand on her smock and then thrusting it into the bag. "The bird cage has turned up! Henry's going to get it back tonight."

"Really?" James raised an amused eyebrow. "You do enjoy all this, don't you, Emily?"

"We want to deliver it to Mrs. Cormorant and get paid, but first we're going to look for clues, like woolly hairs from an overcoat, or— or—"

"Underwear buttons," Henry put in sourly.

"But I forgot, James. You're a suspect, and I shouldn't tell you all. You're invited to a party I'm giving tomorrow night. Just for suspects."

James grinned. "Emily, you're wonderful. I'll bring some liquor, unless you're serving fingerprint ink."

"I'd appreciate the liquor. I'm a little low financially after the cape. James, you didn't see it!" She flung down her brush and yanked the cape from the shelf. "Isn't it elegant?" Did you ever think you would see Emily Murdock in mink? Neither did I. Three hundred dollars."

James whistled. "Must be stolen. Where did you get it?"

Henry told him. "Cassamassima has got himself into something very smelly, I'm afraid. And our Emily, never one to let her conscience interfere with her pleasure, is playing along with him."

"It must be worth a thousand, anyway," James observed, feeling the fur. "Don't let Cornelia see it, or I'll be obliged to pawn my watch and get her one."

Emily said Cornelia wouldn't want one like hers. "You'll tell her about the party and you'll both come, won't you?" she added.

James promised. "Who else will be there?"

"Harmon Delaphine, and Link, and Hilda. Henry and me." She paused. "It isn't a very big party, is it? Oh, I forgot Mrs. Giddings."

Henry protested. "You can't ask her. She's not interested in people like us."

"She's just a lonesome old lady. And since the gun was in her bust—"

"Surely you don't think she had anything to do with the murder?" James asked, horrified. "She comes from one of the best families in Baltimore."

"I'm not asking her as a suspect," Emily explained. "We need another woman to round out the party."

"She won't come," Henry said positively.

"You think so?" Emily smiled. "I've already asked her, and she said yes."

"When did you ask her?"

"Over at Hilda's. She was having a shampoo. You know her own hair is absolutely white, James. Would you ever guess it? I think the transformation is very natural."

"Since when has Mrs. Giddings been having her hair done at Hilda's?"

"I don't know."

"Ever see her in there before?"

Emily bit her lip, thinking. She didn't remember. "But Hilda's very good—lots of people go there."

"Seems like a long trip from Ninety-first Street."

"With a chauffeur?"

A short time after James left Mr. Burgreen came in. Emily told him about her party, and he appeared to be thinking of something else. "That's very nice," he said when she had finished.

"And of course you're invited," Emily added politely.

"Thanks, but I can't go to parties given by customers."

"This is exceptional," Emily insisted.

"I'm sure of it."

"It won't be a success without you. And think of the wonderful opportunity to observe the people who may have killed Mrs. Delaphine."

Burgreen gave her an agreeable smile, sat down on a newspaper covering the stuffings of a moth-eaten sofa, and filled his pipe. "Anything new?" he asked.

"The box," Emily said. "You tell him, Henry."

Henry explained that they had called on Harmon the night before. "Emily stole a little wooden box which she swears was in Mrs. Delaphine's house the night she was killed. Emily says she and Cleo talked about it."

"Did you ask Harmon Delaphine how he got hold of it?"

"No," Emily said. "I knew he'd stolen it. It has a secret drawer, very tiny. The drawer was empty, though. I thought Harmon took it while he was there killing Mrs. Delaphine. Henry says no, Harmon was in her house the other night, looking for things, and he took it then."

"That is, if he didn't kill her," Henry explained.

Burgreen asked to see the box, and Emily said it was in her apartment. "Roscoe can go and get it for you."

"Never mind. I'll see it some other time. No great interest, if it's empty." He sat back, crossed his legs, and watched the drops of muddy water roll off his rubbers. "You two had some weird idea when you went to see Dr. Delaphine," he suggested. "It wasn't just a friendly visit."

Emily said that was right, she wanted to ask him if his patient, Mr. Percy Ford, could have been killed with no digitalis.

"What?" Burgreen sat forward.

Emily explained, in confusing detail.

Burgreen chuckled. "Bound to have another homicide, Miss Murdock?"

"What do you think of the idea?"

"Not much. But keep trying."

"Your chemists of course analyzed the pills found on the body?" Henry inquired.

"There were no pills found on the body," Burgreen told him. "Pillbox empty."

"That makes it harder, doesn't it?" Emily reflected. "Do you think the murderer removed the pills that were left?"

Burgreen said the person who found the body had a chance to do anything she liked.

"What do you mean, she? I didn't touch that horrid little man."

The detective grinned. "Glad to hear it, Miss Murdock. But you may not have been the first to arrive at the scene, you know."

Henry suggested that perhaps Mr. Ford had chanced to die when the pillbox was empty—a great boon to the murderer. Burgreen said that was quite possible.

"Find out anything about my sister's friend, Donald Clark?"

"He exists. He's quite a flashy character, but as far as we can find out he hasn't been away from Los Angeles during the last month. Our information is quite substantial. And he is not related to Mrs. Cleo Delaphine. Perhaps there's another Donald Clark, although frankly I don't think so. Lord tells us he never heard Mrs. Delaphine mention any such relative. He had known her a long time. However, people don't go around talking about down-and-out cousins." He added that they had the records searched in Mrs. Delaphine's native town of Westfield, New Jersey—an orderly, prim, record-keeping town—and nothing had been discovered.

Roscoe offered him shrimp chips from the bag, and Burgreen said they were not on his diet list.

"They're not fattening," Emily told him. "I eat them all the time."

"And look how thin you are," Henry added.

"We'll have them at the party," Emily promised, "and you can eat them then, because who diets at a party?"

Burgreen put on his hat and opened the door.

"What diet do you use?" Emily asked.

"*Harper's Bazaar*," he growled, and went quickly down the stairs.

They were very busy all day, and the brief visit of Cornelia in mid-afternoon was scarcely noticed, although Emily did find time to show her the cape. Henry thought Cornelia looked ill. He disliked his sister, distrusted her, was always glad to see her go, and yet he couldn't help feeling concern for her. Relatives were an unavoidable calamity.

As they were getting ready to close the studio Henry said he thought it would be more convenient to have the party in his apartment. "You haven't cleaned yours for six weeks, have you?" he asked.

Emily was indignant. "You'd think I wallowed. Anyway, your kitchen isn't finished."

"I know. I thought maybe you could be painting the edges of the shelves while I went to look at the bird cage."

"That isn't fair. You have all the fun and I do all the dirty work."

At half-past eight he dropped a pair of wire clippers into his pocket, with a note he had typed, and left Emily grumpily slapping red paint on the edge of the top shelf. She had rolled her cape into a ball and stuffed it into the refrigerator. Cold, she said, was good for fur. And who would think of looking there for a mink?

Henry hailed a taxi at the corner of Sixty-second and told the driver to take the road through Central Park to West Seventieth. It was a clear night, crackling cold, and the lights in the hotels and apartment buildings pricked sharply through the branches of bare trees. He settled back, enjoying the quiet. If Emily were along she would talk every minute.

It was a large cooperative apartment house, and Mrs. Adrian Smith, the name Emily had got from Hilda, was listed under 12-A. The doorman asked the switchboard girl to call Mrs. Smith. "She's not in," the girl reported.

"Doesn't matter. I'm just picking up something for a decorator," Henry said, glad to learn that he would not have to deal directly with the woman.

They let him go up. The maid looked him over dubiously. "She didn't say anything about you taking the bird cage."

"I've got the order here, miss." He handed her the note which he had prepared. "She wants it retouched for Christmas and if I don't get it tonight they can't finish it for her. It's nothing to me one way or the other, miss."

The girl scowled a moment, and then shrugged. "You'll have to take it down. I'm no acrobat." She led him to a large pink-and-blue bedroom where the bird cage had already been hung as a lighting fixture. Henry took off his shoes, stood on a chair, clipped the wire with his shears, and lifted down the cage. There was no doubt that it was the one Emily had decorated.

The buzzer sounded.

"That's her now," the girl said, hurrying out.

Henry glanced wildly round the room. There was nowhere to go so he stayed where he was, listening.

"Never mind, then," a female voice said. "I'll call her tomorrow. Just stopped by. Oh, I wonder if you'd mind showing me the new bedroom light Bella said she'd found?"

"Certainly, Mrs. Giddings," the girl answered.

He'd thought the voice was familiar. "Good evening, Mrs. Giddings," he said as that lady entered the bedroom.

She peered at him in the pale light from the dressing table. "Why, Mr. Bryce," she said, and there was no great pleasure in her voice.

"He's come for the bird cage," the maid explained. "You got here just in time to see it, Mrs. Giddings."

"And why is Mr. Bryce taking the bird cage?"

"We're touching it up for Mrs. Smith," Henry said easily. "It had a rough time, due to accidents beyond our control."

"Young man"—Mrs. Giddings' square blond face was aggressively suspicious—"weren't you doing a bird cage for Mrs. Oliver Cormorant?"

"Yes," Henry said.

"Is this it?"

"I believe so."

"And what do you intend doing with it?"

"As I said, we're retouching it for Mrs. Smith."

Mrs. Giddings turned to the maid. "Would you mind getting me a glass of water, Marie? With ice, please. Plenty of ice."

Marie vanished obediently.

"Now look here, Henry," Mrs. Giddings said in a much lower voice, "I know Mrs. Smith has not asked you to redecorate that absurd cage. You're stealing it."

"Only temporarily," Henry protested.

"What for?" She leaned forward, one freckled hand grasping the arm of the chair. The diamonds on it caught the light. "Do you think the bird cage has something to do with Mrs. Delaphine's death?"

Henry smiled. "In the words of Mr. Durante, 'Everybody wants to get in the act.' We just thought there might be some hairs or something caught in the wires of the cage."

Mrs. Giddings considered this. "If that were possible, I should think the police would have shown an interest."

"They don't know it's here."

"They won't like it when they find you've acted on your own. You'd better reconnect the thing and protect your character."

"My character is beyond help." Henry stood up. "Don't tell Mrs. Smith, will you?"

"I may." She turned round to take the glass of water from Marie, and while she had her face in it Henry picked up the bird cage and left.

Funny old gal, he reflected, riding back through the park. She seemed to know everybody and his dog. Money in buckets. Dangerous to wear rings like that.

He hoped Emily was through painting—she could make a job last a long time if she wanted to keep you awake and talk to you. He went through the vestibule, put his key in the lock of the second door. Someone was coming down the stairs, probably Emily. That was fine. He opened the door. There was no one on the stairs. He went on up. The door to his apartment was propped open with a chair.

"Hi," he called.

"Hello," Emily answered from the kitchen.

"What's the idea of having the door open?"

"It's hot in here, especially up near the ceiling. Did you get it?"

Henry didn't answer at once—he was looking at a glob of mud and water on the polished floor.

"I said, did you get it?" Emily repeated.

"Sure. Mrs. Giddings was there. She knows this Smith woman. She knows 'em all. I hope you went out to get yourself a little refreshment while I was gone."

"Why should I go out? There's plenty of stuff in your refrigerator."

"Oh." Henry examined the wet spot, found two others, went back into the hall, found more. He ran quickly up to the third floor, then to the fourth. He saw no one. "Got out while I was talking to Emily," he said to himself, coming back to the apartment. He didn't like it. Of course it might have been Beardsley Satchel, drunk again, but Beardsley invariably made the noise of a herd of elephants when he was drunk. He didn't say anything to Emily.

She came down off the ladder, wiping her face with a dirty hand and sniffling slightly. He had a moment of great weakness. He pictured

Emily lying here with a knife in her back and he almost put his arms around her. Not quite. He saved himself.

"It is the same one, isn't it!" Emily cried, holding up the bird cage. "Now what do we do?"

Henry said he would go over it with a reading glass, looking for fibers.

"Nice that nobody kept a bird in it while it was missing." Emily turned the cage upside down, gave a shriek. "There's something in it, Henry!"

Neatly taped to the metal at the top on the inside was a piece of green-and-white paper. Henry took a knife, lifted the tape, secured the paper and unfolded it. It bore a pleasant portrait of Mr. Patrick J. Galvin, leaning on a window sill in his native country. "Galvin's Irish Mixture," he read, flushing. "Burgreen."

"You mean he's looked at it and taken away all the evidence and everything?" Emily demanded.

Henry said that was it.

Emily's mouth curved upward. "Henry, did you have quite a time getting the cage?"

"I did."

She leaned on the piano, smiling. "Mr. Burgreen is a very smart man, isn't he?"

There was a heavy thud against the door into the hall.

"What was that?" Emily whispered.

"I didn't hear anything." Henry pulled out the ice tray and began to make drinks.

"Somebody's dead in the hall, Henry." Emily was a pale green.

"Control your enthusiasm." Henry went to the door and found Beardsley Satchel leaning against the opposite wall in a state of advanced happiness.

"Hiya?" Beardsley gurgled. "Gotta drink?"

"You don't need a drink, B.S. Go to bed."

"Oh, come on, don't be a prohibitionist. I have something to discuss with you. A mysterious event."

"We'll discuss it tomorrow." Henry started to close the door, because once Beardsley got in there was no getting him out.

"This hallway is haunted, Henry," Beardsley persisted. "I was sitting quietly on the stairs a while ago when up comes a black shadow, slipping and sliding, and I believe the intention of this shadow was to attain the fourth floor, but when he saw me he vanished. Do you hear? He just vanished."

Henry paused. "Who was he?"

"Ah ha, I struck a chord. Give me just a short shot, Henry, and I'll tell you the whole thing."

Henry gave him his own glass, which he hadn't touched, and continued to block the doorway. "Who was he?" he repeated.

"I don't know," Beardsley admitted, swallowing noisily.

"Are you sure it was a man?" Emily asked, over Henry's shoulder.

"No, not exactly."

Henry wasted another five minutes, but Beardsley had nothing more to tell.

"He's always seeing things," Emily said, when Henry had closed the door. "Why did you bother with him? And that good liquor too."

"If you're ready, I'll take you home."

"You never take me home, Henry. Do you want to get rid of me?" Emily took her cape out of the refrigerator and put it on. Henry followed her out and locked his door. Satchel must have gone back to his apartment because there were sounds of violent quarreling from that region.

"I still think the party is a bad idea, Emily," Henry said as they crossed the empty street. "Let's call it off."

She stopped. "Henry, you're afraid."

"No, I just think it's a bad idea. In the first place, it's not a congenial group of people. Hilda and Cornelia—like opening the tiger cages and saying 'Go get 'em.' "

"You're afraid."

"All right, I'm afraid. And now that I've admitted it, would you mind giving me your cape to keep during the night?"

"What for?" Emily's nose sharpened.

"Maybe Satchel saw a thief on the stairs. Neighborhood's full of them."

"But how do they know I have a mink cape?"

Henry asked if there was anybody from the Hudson to the Potomac who hadn't heard. "Give it to me."

Emily obeyed, and promised to lock her door carefully.

Henry's phone was ringing when he got back to his own apartment.

"I'm scared," Emily wailed. "You've got me so jumpy I hear things."

"That's too bad. Go to bed, hold your ears and shut your eyes and think of a nice, strong man."

"Mr. Burgreen is so far away."

Henry hung up. He wondered if it were the cape someone had come looking for, or if it were something else in his apartment. Emily's idea, he concluded, was a good one even though the cape was beginning to have an aroma of onion and blue cheese, and he put it back in the refrigerator.

He thought about Satchel for a few minutes, undoing his tie and looking at himself in the mirror on the closet door. Satchel was a no-good so-and-so, and murder was possibly a step above wife-beating. But Henry didn't believe that Satchel could command the necessary concentration to kill someone, withdraw unnoticed from the scene, and remain unnoticed for all these days. Satchel didn't care enough about his own life to kill someone else to improve it. You had to want something very much, or be very frightened to kill. Beardsley didn't want anything but liquor, and what could he fear that hadn't happened to him already? Henry paused. "Jail?" he said aloud. "He's never been in jail that I know of."

Chapter 7

HENRY woke with a headache and a sense of foreboding. He turned over and looked at the windows, and decided it was snowing again although you couldn't be sure because the windows hadn't been washed since June. A dry eucalyptus leaf in the vase on the piano rattled in the breeze. Ought to get some fresh flowers for that vase. Ought to get up and begin cleaning the place, with a lady like Mrs. Giddings coming to the party. Why Emily wanted a mass of people around on a Sunday was beyond him.

The phone rang and he picked it up without leaving his bed.

"Are you up, Henry?" Emily's bright, energetic voice hurt his ears.

"No, and I'm not getting up. You can call your little friends and tell 'em not to come."

"Oh no. It's all settled, and I've been out and got the papers so you won't have that work to do today."

"Damned thoughtful of you. I'm serious, Emily. Let's postpone the celebration until after the murder has been solved."

"Some murders are never solved. We might wait till we were keeping our teeth in a glass. Anyway, the party is going to clear things up."

"Suppose someone is stabbed or poisoned or spread around with an ax on my good rug?"

"Are you planning to have cold roast beef, Henry?" she asked. "I think Mr. Burgreen would like that."

"I'm having baked seafood."

Emily said Mr. Burgreen didn't like fish. "I wonder if he has his clothes made to order?" she went on.

"He isn't coming to your damned party anyway," Henry reminded her, beginning to be mildly irritated by this fellow Burgreen. He hung up, closed the windows, shuddered at himself in a mirror, and put water and coffee in the percolator. He opened the refrigerator for an egg, saw that the cape was still there. He put the egg in cold water and lighted the gas under it while he considered the unpleasant matter of the wet spots on the floor. If someone wanted to take something from the apartment, maybe it was a good idea to give them the opportunity of the party. He didn't know what it could be they wanted—certainly not the bird cage, because he felt sure the murderer had had his hands on that and thrown it away.

He watched the water beginning to bubble into the glass knob in the percolator lid and thought about the person who had started down the hall stairway to the front door as he was putting his key in the lock. "Satchel saw somebody," he reflected, "so I didn't imagine it. If he were a stranger, he would have come down, passed me, and gone out. Why not? I would have thought nothing of it."

The egg began to boil and he turned off the gas. "That means it was someone I know. He had been in this apartment, he saw or heard Emily in the kitchen, and he didn't want her to see him. If he had spoken to me on his way out, I'd have assumed he had been looking for me and had spoken to Emily. Natural thing for me to do, then, is to come on up to the apartment, say to Emily, 'I passed so-and-so on his way out. Asked him to come back, but he wouldn't.' Then Emily tells me he hasn't been in here at all. I conclude what? That he didn't want to be seen."

Henry made some toast, turned on the radio, and was delighted to learn that you could now have that Ivory look in a week instead of ten days. He turned it off again, crunching reflectively, and scattering crumbs with the reckless abandon of one who is about to clean his entire dwelling.

"Damn it," he said, in the middle of his second cup of coffee, "if it's somebody I know, I may be having a friendly drink one of these days and drop right out of this world with a snootful of cyanide. I don't like it. I don't know who to trust. Suppose"—he held the idea at the end of a ten-foot mental pole—"suppose it was Emily coming down the stairs? Why wouldn't she want me to see her? Taking something away, maybe? Satchel says he saw somebody sneaking upstairs, but Satchel isn't the most reliable witness I could imagine. Emily could have dashed back into the apartment and started painting before I got here. You're crazy, Bryce," he grunted. "Emily wouldn't kill anybody."

Henry began grubbing. His method was to move everything into the middle of the room, dig out the edges, and then move everything to the edges and go at the center. In the moving everything got a shaking up, and things came to light that had been lost for weeks, such as Emily's blue linen handkerchief, the solitaire deck, a sticky glass from a long-departed old-fashioned, and various sections of the Sunday *Tribune* which Henry had been saving for one reason or another. In honor of Mrs. Giddings he dusted the books, and this entailed a few excursions into Heroditus, a page of Proust in which the poor guy seemed to be all worked up over the price of eggs in Tibet. Cornelia had given him that. Cornelia liked nervous books quivering with problem people. There was a pamphlet Emily had purchased on reading character through handwriting. He glanced through it. "Stupid," he grunted, and sat down on the window sill, the dustrag over his shoulder. Just the sort of thing Emily would fall for. Emily and Cleo Delaphine. "It is practically impossible to disguise one's handwriting," he read. Well, what of it? He wasn't thinking of disguising his handwriting. Anyway, he didn't believe it.

The buzzer sounded. Emily, of course. Henry unlatched the door and got busy.

It was Cornelia. "What on earth are you doing, Henry?" she demanded, holding a handkerchief over her nose.

He explained that important people were expected and sanitary conditions had to be improved.

"I know what you're going to say," Cornelia began, "but I don't think you ought to have this party."

"Why not?"

She looked away from him, running a finger along the edge of the piano. "I just wouldn't have it, that's all."

"You must have some reason."

"You're getting the wrong people together, Henry." Her voice was petulant and she still did not look at him.

"You can put up with Hilda if Mrs. Giddings can."

"You've invited that hairdresser?"

"You don't have to come, Cornelia. More ham for the rest of us."

"I'm coming. James wouldn't miss it for the world. Henry, has it occurred to you that Emily might be involved in these things?"

"What things?"

"These murders."

Henry gave her a look. "I know you don't like Emily, but that's going a little far, even for you, Cornelia. Anyway, so far as I know there has been only one murder."

"I'd love coffee and a toasted muffin," Cornelia said, dropping the subject.

Ordinarily Henry would have told her to go on home and make herself a cup of coffee, but he was curious to know what had made her get out of bed on a snowy Sunday morning and come over here. He dropped the dustcloth and went into the kitchen. "I was just looking at a book on handwriting—it's in the bookcase there. It says you can't completely disguise your own writing. Do you believe that?"

"I don't know," Cornelia answered indifferently.

"Wasn't Cleo interested in that stuff? Seems to me I saw some books around there."

Cornelia didn't say anything, and he thought she hadn't heard. He repeated the question, making conversation.

"Probably something a maid left around," Cornelia said loftily. "I'm sure Cleo never bothered with anything like that."

"I'm sure she did."

"I'm sure she didn't."

"Want to bet?" He came to the doorway with a hot muffin in his hand.

Cornelia was at the bookcase bending over the titles. She moved away quickly. "What makes you so disagreeable this morning, Henry? I knew Cleo very well. You knew her scarcely at all."

"All right." He shrugged. "It's not a matter of life and death. How do you want your coffee—sugar, cream? We have some very nice fresh arsenic this morning."

Cornelia drank three cups of coffee and left, not saying where she was going.

James called after a while and asked about her. "She seemed so jittery when she left the house this morning, Henry. I'm worried."

"She'll be all right," Henry said, comforting him. "She's probably annoying some female friend. Maybe she and Mrs. Giddings are hatching a scandal on Eighty-first Street. See you tonight."

"Righto," James said, but not with his usual heartiness.

Emily came in, bearing a bunch of jonquils and three newspapers. "You're doing a wonderful job, Henry," she said. "I'll help you." She tore the paper off the flowers and dropped it, along with a mass of big tough ferns, in the middle of the floor. "I think they'll look nice in that glass bowl you have."

"That's being used for potato chips."

"You've got plenty of things to put potato chips in." Emily emptied the bowl onto a plate, filled it with water, stuffed the jonquils into it.

"Looks like a bunch of celery," he said, picking up the debris.

"Mother called again this morning," Emily remarked.

"What did she have to say?"

"She thinks I should stop bothering with these murders and get my Christmas shopping done." Emily settled on the couch with the three newspapers and proceeded to make a nest of reading matter. At five o'clock he sent her home to dress and cleared away the papers.

Then Roscoe came, with a big apron and a slight odor of Third Avenue bistro, and they made several trips to the delicatessen.

At half-past six Henry had the table extended and was laying out silver and plates for a buffet supper while Emily watched him and tossed salted nuts into her mouth.

"It really isn't any trouble to have a party, is it?" she remarked.

"I wonder if I could trouble you to hang up that bearskin before people get here?" Henry asked.

Emily decided she didn't want her cape sardined among the common clothes in Henry's one big closet. She hung it from the shower rod in the bathroom.

At seven the buzzer sounded. "Somebody's awfully early," Emily said. "I hope it's Mr. Burgreen."

It was Hilda, smelling fiercely of *Le Tigre*, her hair a lacquered edifice stiff enough to scrape kettles with.

"Hello, Henry," she said with a negligent glance at the table. "What are you having?"

"Baked seafood," Emily told her. "It's wonderful the way Roscoe does it."

"I hate fish. My God, why don't you put some green stuff in that bouquet?" She wrinkled her nose at the jonquils.

"I like them the way they are," Henry stated firmly.

"They'd look like a lot more with something green," Hilda advised. "Didn't they give you any ferns?"

"I threw them away," Emily said peaceably.

Hilda stalked to the garbage can in the kitchen, rescued the ferns, shook the water out of them, and jammed them into the bowl on the table. "Now, I think that looks like something," she said, standing off.

Henry carried the bowl to the kitchen, extracted the ferns, and brought the bowl back. Mrs. Giddings arrived at that moment, and then James and Cornelia, and shortly afterward Link and Dr. Delaphine came along. Hilda was mercifully diluted.

Henry had been a little nervous about Mrs. Giddings, but he need not have been. She settled easily into the company, accepted a drink, and looked brightly around.

"Mr. Bryce, I see you still have the bird cage," she said. "You may thank me for not telling Mrs. Smith."

"Thank you." Henry smiled. "I'll return it tomorrow. But our very bright detective, Mr. Burgreen, had already examined it."

"Is that so?" Mrs. Giddings seemed amused. "Strange how much better the police are at being policemen. You'd think people would learn, but some of them never do. Now when my late husband's bank in Las Vegas was robbed, the police did a wonderful job."

"Las Vegas?" Henry repeated. "I didn't know you had Western connections, Mrs. Giddings."

"Oh yes. Lived there for years. Too damned hot."

"How interesting." Cornelia was attentive behind that weary look.

Mrs. Giddings took a polite little sip of martini. "It appears that everyone here knew Mrs. Delaphine," she remarked. "Does that have any significance?"

"Oh no," Emily said quickly. "It's just a friendly little get-together. Isn't it, Henry?"

"I think Mrs. Giddings is on to you, Emily."

"But I didn't ask you as a suspect," Emily told her earnestly. "You were just an extra woman."

Mrs. Giddings smiled. "I like being an extra woman. Henry, may I have another of your excellent cocktails?"

Hilda sat forward on the couch and fixed Dr. Delaphine with an earnest eye. "Doctor," she said, "what does it mean when you feel an impulse to kill another person?"

Harmon, always a gentleman, cleared his throat, answered amiably, "It demonstrates a certain weakness, I suppose. If you were able to defend yourself, you wouldn't have to kill people, would you?"

Link looked at Harmon out of his sleepy eyes. "What does it mean when you like women, Doctor?"

"Personally, I like clams," Emily said.

At that point Beardsley Satchel pounded on the door and opened it without waiting for an answer. "I smell a party," he said, coming in. "Always room for one more."

"We were just going," Link told him, getting up. "A shame you didn't come sooner, old boy."

Henry tried to edge Beardsley out again, but he was not a man who understood hints. "Martinis," he cried, pushing past Henry and making for an unguarded glass on the piano. He swallowed the drink in one gulp. "Anybody want to sing?" He sat down and played "Chloë" and sang in a thick, heavy voice.

"Isn't he dreadful?" Mrs. Giddings remarked amiably. "Doesn't he have a kennel somewhere?"

Link ran upstairs to get Martha. She came down, her hair in pins, her black dress uneven around the hem and considerably spotted over the stomach. "Darling, come on upstairs; supper's ready," she said in her sad, thin voice.

"Supper's ready here." Beardsley waved at the table. "Plenty for everybody. Henry always has plenty."

"You might as well have a bite, Martha," Emily offered generously. Everybody gave Emily dark looks.

"I'd better get him out," Martha said, with a wistful glance at the steaming casserole Roscoe had brought in.

There was nothing to do but feed them, and Beardsley contrived to swallow an unknown number of other people's drinks as he passed unsteadily around the room. Then he was sick in the bathroom. Link and Roscoe finally got him out and up to his own apartment, and made Martha promise to keep him locked in.

"You dope," Henry said to Emily when everyone had gone home. "I ought to beat you. Asking them to have supper with us!"

"You let him in. Anyway, what's the difference?" Emily shrugged. "Every party has some little defect. I honestly thought Mr. Burgreen would come."

"I'm sick of Burgreen." Henry dumped ash trays into a wastebasket. "Why don't you go and live with the guy?"

"I think he's married."

"That's quibbling." He went on gathering up debris and Emily took her compact into the bathroom. She came out with the cape over her arm.

"Lining's coming out of it already," Henry said disagreeably. "You're the most careless person I know."

"Where?"

He pointed out a hanging edge.

Emily flung the cape open. "I don't see how I could have done that. Henry, I think the thread was cut."

"Anything for an alibi. You caught it on a nail." He looked at the ends of the silk thread which held the lining in place. Emily was right—the ends were sharp, not raveled as they would be from a tear. Someone had taken a scissors or a razor and deliberately cut the thread.

"Beardsley," Emily decided. "It's just the sort of trick he would play."

"Where was your cape during the party?"

"In the bathroom."

"Beardsley was pretty busy while he was in there."

"Disgusting drunk. Why don't they lock him up?"

Henry looked through her, thinking. "I imagine everybody was in there during the course of the evening."

"But no one else would do a thing like that, Henry."

"If they were looking for something in the coat they might."

"Looking for something?" Emily fingered the cape nervously. "What?"

Henry shrugged. "I thought when we were at Harmon's the other evening he had a very funny look when he saw the cape. As if he recognized it." He took the cape, examined it carefully, turned the pocket inside out. "Doesn't it look to you as if there had been initials or something embroidered here and ripped off?"

Emily looked closely. "You're right, Henry! Where's your reading glass?" He handed it to her.

"The initials were C.D.," Emily said, her eyes round and scared. "Cleo Delaphine, Henry."

"We'd better tell Burgreen right now." He got the detective at home after calling the station. "You missed a very good party," Henry told him. "Emily's mink cape has been cut open. We think someone was looking for something."

"You mean the papers from the Kremlin?" Burgreen inquired.

"I'm serious. Someone cut the stitching. Cape was in the bathroom during the party. Anyone could have done it."

"Some drunks have destructive tendencies." Burgreen asked laconically who was there, and Henry told him. "Interesting," he conceded. "But it can wait until tomorrow. Good-by."

"Wait a minute—how did you find out Mrs. Smith had the bird cage?"

Burgreen chuckled. "Your friend Hilda the hairdresser. Called me after Miss Murdock had been there to be curled."

Henry said "Oh," and hung up. "I didn't tell him about the initials," he remembered. "Well, he wouldn't find that surprising." He began to gather glasses from the strange places where people managed to leave them during a party.

"I'll wash the dishes," Emily offered.

"Okay, go ahead."

"You mean you want me to?"

"And get the sugar out of the cups." Henry stretched on the couch, groaned once, and shut his eyes.

"But you never want me to do the dishes, Henry. I don't get them clean."

"Stop stalling. You offered. I want to think."

She gave up, and with a great deal of clatter and some muttering to herself she managed to collect most of the stuff and put it through what she fondly called a cleansing process. Henry was thinking about the cape. He didn't think it was an aimless act of vandalism, this cutting the lining.

"If the cape belonged to Cleo Delaphine, how did Cassamassima get hold of it?" he asked out loud.

"She took it to him to be cleaned or mended or something," Emily said, coming to the doorway with a dripping cup.

"It looks new," Henry objected. "Why would she have a new cape cleaned or mended?"

"You can't tell, Henry, whether it's new or not. They do marvelous things with old furs."

"Here's another thing. Suppose it isn't new and she was having it cleaned or remodeled or something. Why have that done in midwinter when she ought to be wearing it? People with any brains have their furs tended to in the summer or early fall."

Emily had to agree. She went on wiping the cup. She wiped the handle off it. "Henry," she said, "Mrs. Delaphine sent the coat to Cassamassima to hide something—something in the lining."

"Not bad, not bad. Assuming that there *was* something in the lining."

"Now"—Emily came over and sat down facing him, the wet dish-towel over her knees—"what was she hiding?"

"That, my dear girl, is what nobody knows."

"Somebody knows. They probably have it right now." Emily looked around the room, shivered slightly. "One of those people, Henry—do you realize that? And suppose they'd decided to kill me to get the cape?"

Henry, remembering last night and the wet tracks on his floor, thought that possibly someone had been tempted to do just that, but for some reason had changed his mind. Or her mind.

"If Cleo's death and this cape business are tied up," he went on thoughtfully, "then she was killed because she had some information— she had the goods on somebody."

"What goods?" Emily demanded practically.

"What skulduggery has been going on lately?"

"Mrs. Delaphine was murdered, that's all I can think of."

"Obviously she didn't send the cape to Cassamassima after she was dead. It wasn't her own death she knew about, Emily."

"I suppose not." Emily's white brow became furrowed. "There's that Las Vegas thing," she offered somewhat timidly.

Henry sat up, surprised. "Sometimes you do seem to have a brain. If Cleo knew who pulled that deal, she had the power to ruin someone."

"If she knew, she'd tell the police, wouldn't she?" Emily objected.

"Not if she needed money, and thought she would be paid for keeping quiet."

"That's blackmail. Mrs. Delaphine wouldn't be a blackmailer."

"Why not?" Henry demanded.

"You have to be part of the underworld to do that."

"Listen, child, every stratum has its bottom side. And from what we knew of Mrs. Delaphine, she had some rather small traits." Henry paused, staring at the ceiling. "If Delaphine knew, and if somebody had to kill her, then she had proof, Emily. And the proof was in your cape."

"Maybe she just guessed," Emily suggested, "and it was the right guess, and they shot her, bang like that, without any second thoughts."

"Maybe. But I don't think it was a guess. First, Mrs. Delaphine got one of those letters from Las Vegas. We know that. What else do we know about her?"

"She was stingy. She liked lettuce."

Henry wasn't listening. His eye fell on the handwriting book he and Cornelia had discussed that morning. "Didn't Cleo have a hanger-on who was supposed to be a handwriting expert?"

"Yes." Emily nodded. "When we were doing work for her—before she got the divorce from Harmon. She talked about it all the time."

"I thought so. Cornelia didn't remember anything about it. Well, as we were saying, Cleo got one of those letters supposed to be signed by James. Tie that to her interest in handwriting and what do you get?"

Emily returned his gaze blankly. "I don't know. What?"

"She found out whose signature it really was. Either alone, or with the help of an expert."

Emily frowned. "Then all our ideas about who killed her are wrong, Henry. Because the mining deal was pulled by someone we don't know—a professional crook."

"Who told you that? We've been assuming that, but it isn't necessarily so at all. Look, who would find it easier to send a letter like that to a list of James' friends than someone who knew him very well, was informed of his travel plans, and was acquainted with the financial status of his friends? Now how did Cleo know who it was? She must have had other handwriting done by the person who signed the Las Vegas letters with James' name. Therefore, it was someone she knew and received notes from."

"That lets out Link. He never would have written to Cleo—he didn't like her."

"You mean you've been suspecting Link?"

"Well—a little."

"He's sold things to Cleo. When you sell something you send a bill. Link writes his bills in longhand, Emily." Henry went on slowly, "She also undoubtedly had samples of Harmon's writing."

"And Cornelia's," Emily said a little too eagerly.

"And Cornelia's."

"But why would one of James' friends do a thing like that, Henry? It would be awfully dirty."

"Needed money."

"Cornelia's always interested in money. She had the best chance to do it, too, and we all know her principles."

"I'd like to hear what Burgreen has to say. Well, he'll be at the studio in the morning."

"Do you think so?" Emily asked hopefully. "In that case I'll go home now and get some sleep, otherwise I'll look like an old hag."

"What makes you think you won't anyway? I'll walk over with you."

"I wish you'd keep the cape, Henry. It makes me nervous."

"No danger attached to it now. If there was anything in the lining they have it."

"I suppose you're right," she said doubtfully, and put it on. Henry took her across the street, came back, looked at the havoc in the kitchen, and went to bed. If he ever had to marry Emily he hoped they would be able to keep a slave.

He was on the edge of sleep when the phone rang. Thinking it was Emily being frightened again, he didn't answer at once. Then, uneasy, he took it off the cradle.

"Henry?" James asked. "Awfully sorry to bother you—hope you weren't asleep?"

"It's all right, Beansie. What's on your mind?"

"You'll think I'm mad, I suppose. But all of a sudden I had the idea that maybe Cleo Delaphine knew who swindled my friends." He paused hopefully.

"Umm," Henry grunted.

"You don't think much of it, eh?" James cleared his throat apologetically. "Sort of improbable, I grant you. But the Las Vegas trick is constantly in my mind, so it was bound to connect itself sooner or later with Cleo's death."

"Where did Mrs. Delaphine get her divorce?" Henry inquired.

"She didn't get it. Harmon did. Confidentially, she put up an awful fight. But he finally got rid of her and paid a very decent alimony too. I believe he went to Nevada."

Henry said that was very interesting. He decided to tell James about Emily's cape. "Someone took a razor or something and cut the threads of the lining while the party was going on."

"What?" James was horrified. "What reason could they have had? Henry, you know what I think? That cape was not new—I've been trying to place it in my mind ever since Emily showed it to me. And I think now it belonged to Cleo."

"That's what we decided when we found the initials C.D. in the lining. I wonder who else knew it?" Henry paused and lighted a cigarette which tasted like burning feathers. "Have you known Mrs. Giddings a long time, Beansie?"

"No. I can't say I know her at all well, really. She and Cornelia see something of each other." He added doubtfully, "You aren't trying to tie her into things?"

"She seems to have developed a sudden and unexplained interest in our activities," Henry muttered.

James pointed out Mrs. Giddings' eminent respectability, her extremely honest and forthright appearance, and her apparent lack of connection with Cleo Delaphine. "They were never intimate friends," he added. "Merely acquaintances, as far as I know. Well, I won't keep you from your rest any longer, Bryce. But I wish they'd clear up the whole damned business. It's making Cornelia frightfully jumpy. Wouldn't it be a good break for the rest of us if they found this mysterious Donald Clark did it? I'd feel sorry for him, of course, but you don't feel nearly as sorry if you don't know the person. Sometimes I wonder, though, if this fellow really exists. Seems damned odd to me she never mentioned him. Ashamed of him, maybe."

Finally James rang off, and Henry mangled the cigarette and went to sleep.

Emily did not go to sleep. She lay awake thinking, partly because the room was stuffy. Of course no one could get in the front windows, but all the same it was safer to have them closed. Inside her lower berth it was warm. She tossed the feather quilt to the floor, ripped off a blanket, turned over her pillow. It was still too warm. She got up and changed from flannel to silk pajamas, walked around the room a few times, in and out of the obstacles. The cape business had upset her terribly. It was coming close to your person when they began cutting up your clothes. She fell back on the bunk, lay there with her arms under her head, and stared at the bamboo blinds. Slits of street light made a thin pattern on the screen across the room and on the walls.

Suddenly she knew who had killed Cleo Delaphine. She had no idea how she had arrived at this knowledge, but she had it, and it was terrifying. She tiptoed to the window, moved the blind aside, and looked down into the dark street. Everything down there was immensely sharper, larger, darker. She dropped the blind again, turned back into the room, stumbled over the rug, and put her hand on the phone. Suppose she didn't tell? Suppose she was the only one who knew, and she didn't tell? Was it so awful for a person to get away with a murder? If they really had to kill somebody, and never did again?

She sat on the edge of the berth in a sort of stupor, her mind racing here and there to gather the threads of the pattern. Everything fitted together—too well. She went over it and over it, trying to find a flaw. There was none, so far as she could see. If only she could tell someone. She had never been able to keep information to herself, and this was such a monstrous thing to keep in her head.

She went to the kitchenette and rinsed the coffee from a cup she had used at breakfast, put the teakettle on, and leaned on the sink, waiting for it to boil. Her hands and feet were ice-cold and damp. The electric clock made a muttering sound. It was ten minutes after three. If only she could tell Henry. She always told Henry, and he with a laugh reduced a thing to its proper size, so you weren't frightened any more. The water boiled, she poured some over a little mound of instant coffee, and stirred it absently with a fork.

The coffee had a warming effect, but it made her feel more than ever like a wound-up cat.

She had to tell someone. She simply had to. She went to the phone and gave her mother's number in Babylon. She could see her mother fumbling for her slippers, struggling into her purple silk dressing gown, finding the hall light, and plumping down the stairs muttering to herself, "All right, all right, I'm coming." Finally there was an indignant "Hello" on the line.

"Mother," Emily whispered, "I'm coming out. Leave the door open for me, will you?"

"Coming out? Tonight?"

"Yes, right now."

"Emily, are you crazy?"

Emily said she had to come—there was something she had to tell someone.

"I'd just as soon you told somebody else," her mother said. "Do you know what time it is?"

"No."

"You'll never get a train. You'll just sit down there in that cold station till morning. Where's Henry? Why don't you call him?"

"I can't."

"What do you mean, you can't?"

"Mother, just take me at face value, will you? I'm coming. Goodby." Emily hung up.

She dressed, feeling wretched, took out her cloth coat, and hesitated. Her mother hadn't seen the mink cape. She put it on, dumped the contents of two pocketbooks together, hoping the essentials would be there, and let herself out.

There was a strange deadness in the city at this hour. Not even a drunk going home. No milkman's horse clop-clopping comfortably over the pavement. Nobody at all, just a blank street, and a heavy choking smell of coal gas and foul East River wind. No lights in the buildings except the dim, economical small bulbs in hallways, waiting for the janitors to come and turn them off at daylight. Emily shivered, hurrying toward Lexington Avenue. She walked a block without seeing a cab, and considered taking a subway although it would be dank and desolate down there with possibly a drunk or two sleeping lengthwise on the seats.

"Maybe I ought to go back," she thought, her teeth chattering, her bare arms wound tightly in the inadequate fur. Then a cab came puttering down the avenue, saw her, slowed. "Taxi, miss?"

"Yes," she said, and got in gratefully. The driver's name was Samson. She felt better.

They went through several red lights and nobody was there to care. The city hadn't even begun to stretch before getting out of bed. They approached the great gray shape of the Pennsylvania Terminal. "You want the Long Island side?" Samson asked.

"Yes, please."

"You think you're gonna get a train?"

"I hope so."

"You're not. There's nothin' till six twenty-five." He talked just like her mother. It was monotonous, Emily reflected, the way everyone treated her as if she were a child. "What are you going to do around here for three hours all by yourself? You better wait upstairs, there's more people up there."

"I'll be all right," Emily said haughtily, paid him, and walked away. It wasn't exactly what she had planned, but now that she was here she wasn't going back to the apartment. She descended the iron stairway, walked along the usually busy arcade, now silent and empty. The drugstore was closed, and even the small lunch bars. Bottles gleamed in the liquor-store window but no one was being tempted. She entered the overheated small waiting room, sat down on a dingy brown wooden bench. There were three other people, a man and girl left over from a night club and a man mopping the floor. Emily sat still for some time. The clock hands didn't seem to move at all. The droning voice of the girl faded into the echoing spaces of the room. The man with the bucket washed his way to the farthest door and disappeared. Then Emily seemed to see Link and Henry making up a batch of purple capsules. Mrs. Giddings stood behind them, scowling. Henry pulled a hypo from his vest pocket and stuck it in Mrs. Giddings' arm. She snatched it out indignantly.

Emily's neck snapped and she woke up. The man and girl were gone. She was the only person in the waiting room. There ought to be a policeman walking through, but there never was when you wanted to see one. The clock hand had moved twenty-five minutes.

You couldn't see over the backs of the benches unless you stood up.

She was going to stand up—she was going to get out of this room. She waited a moment, listening. It seemed to Emily that someone else was breathing, not far away. Cautious breathing, slightly asthmatic. Or perhaps they had a cold.

She clutched her cape about her and stood up, looked quickly around. She could see no one. She ran to the door, jerked it open, hurried along the arcade to a passageway with an arrow and a sign "Pennsylvania Waiting Room." As soon as you left the arcade things became shabby and darker, and you noticed the musty smell of railroad. She climbed the steel-and-concrete stairway, not stopping to listen and yet certain that someone else had come along that passage and was waiting for her to get to the top of the stairs so that he could climb them.

Her knees quivering, she came out into the light and activity of the upper terminal, crossed the high vaulted area where the trains were posted, and entered the women's side of the main waiting room. Lots of people were waiting, in states ranging from sleep to nervous collapse, and a baby was crying. It was a very comfortable sound. Emily sat down and faced the door through which she had come. No one she knew appeared in that doorway. If they had followed her, they weren't coming in here after her.

She had opened her handbag and taken out her compact when someone said, "Emily, what the hell are you doing here?"

She started. "Why, Link!"

"Your mother called me. She said you were down here waiting for a Long Island train and would I please rescue you. What's the idea?" He dropped into the seat beside her and yawned mightily. He hadn't taken time to wash his face or brush up and he really looked awful—like something left in an alley.

"Link"—Emily faced him earnestly—"I want you to tell me the truth. I won't give you away. Were you following me just now—from the Long Island waiting room?"

"What?" He looked incredulous, then he laughed. "Why should I get out of a nice warm bed to follow you around Penn Station when I can see you any day in the week in comfort?"

"What did my mother say?"

"She implied that Emily was off again and needed a masculine arm."

"No, I mean what did she say exactly?"

He looked at her. "Are you testing me? Emily, you don't really think I'm making this up?"

"No, of course not. Link, have you ten dollars? I'd like to take a cab out to Babylon. That's what I should have done in the first place, but I didn't have enough money with me."

Link said she ought to go home and go to bed, but he pulled out a twenty-dollar bill and gave it to her. "Your mother would like it better if I went with you."

Emily cleared her throat nervously, opened her bag, and put the bill in her wallet. "I don't want to hurt your feelings, Link, but I'd rather you didn't come along."

"Whatever you say. I'll put you in a cab, but first let me buy you a drink or a cup of coffee."

They went into the Savarin.

"I see you're wearing the famous fur piece," Link observed. "May I have the honor of hanging it on a hook for you?"

She let him take it. "You know what happened at the party, Link?" she asked. "Somebody ripped open the lining."

"I'll be damned," he said, looking at it. "Sure you didn't catch the thread on something and rip it yourself?"

"Don't be silly. I'm very careful of that cape. I think it was a man, because a woman would have sewed it up again."

Link smiled. "In your book a criminal comes completely equipped from sewing kit to purple poison. Even a woman might not have a needle and thread in her bosom, you know." He paused. "And some men, like Bryce, are pretty handy with a needle."

"What made you say that?" she asked quickly, picking up the steaming cup of coffee and burning her mouth.

"I don't know. Any reason why I shouldn't say that? Emily, I wish you'd go home. You look beat."

She got away finally, and found herself alone in a cab speeding through the sleeping population of the island toward Babylon. She didn't want to think, so she studied the stubby red neck of the driver. He made funny noises, like a Teddy bear with a whistle inside, and she wondered how long it would be before he cracked up. Perhaps not tonight, she decided hopefully. It must be very wearing to be a taxi driver. Ordinarily she spoke to them, and asked about their children, but she maintained a careful silence with Mr. Bolivar Bubinsky, feeling that that was safer.

After they had left Jamaica she began to notice the headlights behind them. At a distance, but a steady distance. When Bubinsky slowed, the other car slowed. "I give up," Emily said to herself. "I can't take any more tonight. If they're following me, let them follow me. Let them cut me up and leave me in chunks in some lonely field. If only they kill me before they cut me up."

They reached the outskirts of Babylon, still with the other car behind them, went through the town, turned into her mother's street. Emily paid the driver and ran up the steps. There was a light in the dining room. She put her thumb on the bell and kept it there. The lights of the other car came slowly down the street as Bubinsky drove off. It was a yellow cab. It didn't stop, but continued to the end of the block, turned off, and disappeared. Emily's mother opened the door.

"Well," she said. "It's about time."

Chapter 8

HENRY went down to Fifty-first Street to talk to Burgreen before going
to the studio. The detective had a bright-eyed, well-rested look and he
was reading the Monday-morning papers with the utmost relaxation.

"Hello, Bryce," he said, with a trace of irritation as if Henry reminded him of unpleasant duties.

"We found the marks of initials which had been ripped out of Emily's
cape. C.D.," Henry announced, sitting down without being asked.

"So you two bright young things think that Mrs. Delaphine was hiding her last will in this fur article and that I should tear around the
country to see who took it during your brawl last night?" Burgreen tilted
his chair back on two legs.

"As a matter of fact I had something quite different in mind," Henry
said. "I wondered if you would consider telling me what you found out
from Bailey and Rousseau of Boston?"

Burgreen snorted. "Glad to tell you, Bryce. Absolutely nothing. I
may add that Bailey and Rousseau are the most completely inactive,
doddering, pigheaded, blue-blooded private dicks which it has ever been
my lot to come across. For them any event which takes place in New
York is immediately filed under 'unimportant and in poor taste.' States
beyond the Mississippi are in a sort of dream world for them. Nevada is
Indian territory. They wouldn't tell him so, but they feel that James was

147

out of his mind to venture into that part of these barbarous United States and anything which happened to him as a consequence of that hot-blooded trip was only what he deserved."

Henry said James had given him to understand that Bailey and Rousseau were the last word in brains and reliability. "But where Boston is concerned, James is a little prejudiced," he added.

"They're reliable in the sense that you will always find them at the same address. They've grown fast to the floor. They're sessile, if you know what that means."

Henry said he would look it up. "They let you see the material James turned over to them in connection with the Las Vegas deal, I suppose?"

Burgreen frowned. "I've been wasting phone calls on them for the last week trying to get one of the letters the crook sent to Lord's friends. They did send me copies of the answering telegrams wiring the money. But they say they don't have the letters. James says they do have—that he turned the whole business over to them. I haven't been in their offices, but from my dealings with them I wouldn't be surprised if the letters were filed in an old teapot."

"If you've gone to all this trouble you must have thought there was some connection between the murder of Mrs. Delaphine and the swindle in Las Vegas," Henry suggested.

Burgreen said he had to try to track down all the unusual aspects of any case. "However," he added agreeably, "nothing has turned up which confirms the idea of a connection there." He gave Henry one of his suspiciously open smiles as he took out his tobacco box and filled his pipe. "What do you think?"

"I don't know."

"I like this fellow Satchel as a murderer," Burgreen went on affably. "Imagine how glad his wife would be to get rid of him."

"She wouldn't, though," Henry told him. "Martha's life revolves around Satchel's misbehavior. It's her whole existence. If he suddenly became a model character I think she'd be damned sore."

"Satchel's firm was doing business for Mrs. Delaphine—very small amount. Beardsley had been handling her account, but they told me down there that she asked to be transferred to someone else—didn't like him. Can't blame her." Burgreen grinned suddenly. "Can you tell me why I'm giving you all this dope, Bryce?"

"Because I'm such a nice fellow." Henry looked at his watch. "I'll be decapitated. So long." He hurried down to the street, hopped a bus, and arrived at the studio.

Roscoe was there but Emily had not come in. He called her apartment, got no answer. She wasn't at Gottlieb's either. He was about to call Burgreen when she walked in, looking haggard.

"Where have you been?" he asked.

"Good morning," Emily said formally. There was something different about her.

"Mr. Bryce have a fit when he see you not here," Roscoe offered. "Phone all over."

"Is that so? What are you working on this morning, Roscoe?"

"Emily," Henry interrupted, "what's the matter with you?"

"Me? Nothing. Nothing at all. Roscoe, you'd better finish the coffee table first so we can get it out of here."

Henry took fifty cents from his pants pocket. "Roscoe, go down and get me a container of coffee and a doughnut, will you?"

"Sure," Roscoe said, grinning.

"Look here, Henry, I told him to finish that table."

Roscoe was already halfway down the stairs.

"I wanted to talk to you. Has anything happened?"

"No. Everything's all right."

Henry took her arm, turned her toward the light. "You didn't sleep very well."

"I didn't sleep at all." Emily gave him a look which he was at a loss to interpret and went back to the washroom to get into her smock. He followed her halfway.

"What on earth is the matter with you?" he demanded. "You act like a cat trying to conceal oncoming kittens."

"Nothing's the matter with me, I told you, and I'm not going to have kittens. Go away."

Henry went back to the windows and set to work striping chairs. Women were incalculable, he told himself. But Emily wasn't in the habit of keeping anything to herself. This must be tremendous. However, he learned that if you dropped a subject presently Emily herself brought it up—she couldn't contain a secret for more than three hours without bursting.

This time he was wrong—Emily disclosed nothing during the remainder of the morning. She went out for lunch alone—something she almost never did—and when she came back she was more silent and dismal than before.

Roscoe asked if he could have the afternoon off for Christmas shopping and Emily said yes in a dispirited way.

"You done no shopping yourself, Miss Murdock," he reminded her. "You better go soon. All the junk's gonna be gone."

"Tomorrow's Christmas Eve," Henry added. "I haven't bought you anything, Emily. Do you want a comb and brush set or a quilted dressing gown or some stinking soap?"

"Nothing," Emily said. "I'm not going to enjoy this Christmas."

"You shouldn't talk like that, Miss Murdock," Roscoe scolded. "I know what I get you." His face cleared. He took his wallet from his frayed back pocket and counted his money.

"Is the company giving a bonus so I can buy the boss a present too?" Henry inquired.

Emily wouldn't smile. "Henry, why don't you take the afternoon off?" she suggested.

"I thought you wanted me to do the damned Japanese table for Mrs. Lanz?" It had to be repaired and polished and he didn't anticipate the job with any pleasure.

"I'll do it myself," she said. "I can do it better anyway."

"My feelings," Henry protested. "Well, have a good time eating worms."

Henry ambled down the stairs, walked into Link's shop.

"Something's eating Emily," he said. "She's keeping a secret and it's killing her."

"She was pretty weird last night," Link told him.

"You mean at the party?"

"No. Down in Penn Station."

Henry blinked. "She didn't say anything about Penn Station."

Link was surprised. "She didn't tell you she went out to Babylon last night? Her mother called me and asked me to go down and see what Emily was doing. Emily told her she was getting a train, but Mrs. Murdock said there wasn't any train till six-thirty. She was quite worked up. I gave Emily twenty dollars so she could take a taxi—she'd gotten a little tired of waiting by that time. She also had the idea somebody was following her. You know what I think? I think Emily believes she knows who killed Delaphine."

"I'm afraid you're right."

"You don't think she really knows, do you?"

Henry raised an eyebrow, leaning on a case and looking at a tiny gun in a velvet box. "Sometimes Emily's mind, being delightfully unencumbered with logic, arrives at a solution without apparently having touched the problem. This might be one of those times."

James came in, carrying a couple of Christmas packages and looking very cheerful. "Left some of it till the last minute, as usual," he said. "Lucky, though. Found just the bracelet Cornelia wanted in a little shop on Madison. Like to see it?"

Link said sure, but Henry thought he'd better be on his way if he were to get his own shopping done. He walked over to Fifth Avenue, thinking about Emily. If she thought she knew who the murderer was, the idea wasn't making her very happy.

He hopped a bus going downtown, climbed to the upper deck, and lit a cigarette. It was a beautiful sunny day and there would be millions of desperate people converging on the stores. Everybody who had left Aunt Hattie till the last minute would be shoving up to a counter. He was a fool to try, but he had to get something for Emily. At Thirty-ninth Street, in spite of the smear of human beings all over the sidewalk, he took the plunge, fought his way through the crowd into Lord & Taylor's, and immediately felt like a sheet of steel on a Ford conveyor belt. He wondered what shape he would be when he emerged. Carried along on the surge of determined and desperate bodies, he caught glimpses of distant merchandise but was unable to reach any of it. Once he looked up to see gossamer angels floating over his head, and three woman bellowed, "Look where you're going, young man!"

"Oh, Lord, of Lord & Taylor," he muttered, "get me to the perfume counter."

"May I help you, sir?" a young lady asked sympathetically.

"Anything," Henry gasped. "Just so it's a nice bottle."

She held up something which was obscured by a long nose and a feather. He said, "That's fine," and dug for his wallet, trying not to make the creature in the feather think he was pinching her. While he waited for his change and the package he stood tightly against the counter bucking the will of the majority.

"Oh, Mr. Lord and Henry Ford," he said to himself, "were crushed to death by a fighting horde—" He stopped, forgetting the rhyme.

The girl gave him his change. "Something wrong, sir?"

"No. No, that's fine, thanks." Henry seized the bottle, fought his way to Fifth Avenue, flagged a cab, and sat stiffly gripping the package with cold hands as they screeched across Fortieth and tore up Park.

"I'm in a hurry," he kept saying. "Can't you make it any faster?"

In front of the studio he paid the man off, gave him some extra change. "Go into that drugstore and call the Fifty-first Street station. Ask for Detective Burgreen and tell him to get to this address as fast he knows how. If he isn't there, any cop will do." He tore up the studio stairs, flung open the door. He felt a little silly. It was a very peaceful, pleasant scene. Emily was unwrapping her favorite afternoon snack, a half-dozen clams. James was sitting comfortably in an armchair, smoking and reading the *World-Telegram*.

"Hello," Emily said in a sad voice. "You weren't gone very long." She reached for one of the clams.

"Wait," Henry said, taking the shell from her hand and replacing it on the paper plate. "We're having a little Christmas Eve celebration. I brought some brandy—five thousand years old." He shook the perfume bottle. "I'll call Cornelia and Link and we'll have some fun."

"Cornelia?" Emily wrinkled her nose. "It isn't Christmas Eve, Henry. It's only the twenty-third."

James looked at him over the paper. "He must be maddened by the Christmas throng."

Henry dialed the Lord apartment, got his sister, told her to jump in a cab and come over. She made no objection—there was a sort of resignation in her voice. He called Link and told him to come up. Link asked what for, and Henry said never mind, come on. He put down the phone, leaned against the desk, smiling. "Think it's going to snow?" he asked.

"Henry, what's the matter with you? Are you cockeyed?" Emily asked, again reaching for a clam.

"Don't be a pig." Henry took it from her. "We'll all have some later."

Link came in. "What's up?" he asked. "I thought you went shopping."

"I did. And what a buy! Have you been in Lord & Taylor's lately? You wouldn't believe— Ah, here's Cornelia. Now we can begin. Take off your coat, my dear. Make yourself comfortable and have a clam."

Cornelia looked at her husband. James shrugged, folding his paper. "Henry's been shopping." He smiled. "It seems to have affected his mind, but we're all humoring him."

"Have one," Henry said, holding out the paper plate of clams to Cornelia.

"I don't really care for them," she said, "but if you insist—" She picked up one.

James turned a queer gray. "You don't like clams, Cornelia," he said.

"She's going to eat one just to celebrate Christmas Eve," Henry told him. "Aren't you, dear?"

"If it makes you happy." Cornelia lifted the shell to her mouth.

James was out of his chair and had knocked it from her hand before any of them realized what he was doing. He reached into his pocket, came out with a gun, and backed toward the door, pulling Cornelia with him.

The door opened behind him, and Burgreen and McNulty seized his wrists. The gun dropped to the floor.

"Having a party?" Burgreen inquired, leading James to a chair and sitting him down firmly.

Cornelia began a beautiful case of hysterics, and Henry slapped her. Link and Emily stood there with their mouths open, and finally Emily said, "What's wrong with the clams?"

"They're poisoned, especially for you," Henry told her. "Somebody told James you knew who killed Mrs. Delaphine. So he was about to kill you."

Burgreen had picked up the gun and was comparing the number with something in his notebook. "It's your gun, Mrs. Lord," he said. He had a chagrined smile, just for a moment. "I didn't think for a minute he'd try it again. But I reckoned without Miss Murdock. Who told him she knew?"

"I did," Link admitted, bewildered. "I was just kidding. Gosh, Emily, I'm sorry. I had no idea it was Lord."

"That's all right, Link. I don't believe it anyway. You weren't going to poison me, were you, Beansie?"

"I was planning to wind it up in an orderly manner," Burgreen interrupted. "I don't like this dramatic stuff."

"In the decorating business," Link told him, "you don't do anything in an orderly manner. You take what comes. Henry, what gave you the idea the clams weren't kosher?"

"Yes, Henry," Cornelia put in, "you aren't usually very quick. How did you know?"

"Everybody has such lovely bouquets for my intelligence. It was Lord & Taylor that told me. It occurred to me, while I was being slowly pulverized between man-eating female shoppers, that Lord and Ford were very similar names. On a package one might be mistaken for the other. We saw Mr. Ford examining a package in the window of the Thinkers' Club as if he didn't know what was in it. Lord's name was on that package, and it contained the gun. He checked it there for safe keeping after he got it from Roscoe."

Burgreen turned to James, who looked older and very tired. "That right?"

"Quite," James said. "When I asked for the package, the clerk, a very conversational fellow at times, told me he had given it by mistake to Mr. Percy Ford, who also had something in the safe at the time. I asked Ford about it, and he said he had not opened the package, but he looked scared. I was pretty sure he knew what was in it. I couldn't afford to take a chance."

"So you killed him with purple poison," Emily finished.

"Tenacious, isn't she?" Burgreen smiled. "We told you, I believe, that the purple had nothing to do with Ford's death." He turned to James again. "You substituted some harmless palliative for Ford's digitalis, knowing that in due course the lack of his accustomed medicine would prove fatal. But we're going at the thing backwards. Ford's death was an unfortunate afterthought."

"Yes," Emily said, helping Mr. Burgreen. "His big project was killing off Mrs. Delaphine. But why?"

"He had to kill her." Henry sat on the edge of a table. "Mrs. Delaphine knew that it was James himself who had swindled all his friends."

"What?" Emily turned to James. "That isn't true, is it, Beansie? It can't be—you're so painfully honest."

James shrugged. "I've been a lot of things, I'm afraid, Emily dear. I'm glad it's over."

Henry went on. "The handwriting business should have given me an idea. Cleo had discovered and probably verified with an expert that the signature on the letter she got from Las Vegas was James' own. She wouldn't give up her letter, as the others had meekly done, when James said his firm of detectives needed them. James was able to collect all the letters but that one. When Cleo decided to blackmail James, she told him she had proof, and then for safekeeping she put the letter in her fur cape and stored the cape with Cassamassima. When Joe heard she was dead, he thought he'd turn over an honest dollar and sell the cape. He never writes a receipt so you can tell what it's for—he could say she had a fox scarf in his place and turn one back, if necessary."

Burgreen had filled his pipe. "Fairly good so far, Bryce."

"I think it's wonderful," Emily said. "Imagine all that going on in your little old head, Henry, and you never told anybody."

Henry said it had only been going on for about a half-hour and during that time he had been too busy to tell anybody anything.

"Cleo's plan to blackmail James," Cornelia said, "was a very foolish idea, because he couldn't pay her off—we'd spent most of the money. He told me he'd made it in the market."

"I'd like to hear Mr. Lord's version of this," Burgreen suggested.

"As Cornelia says, we had spent most of the money. I let her have all she wanted—"

"And she always wanted a lot," Link put in sourly.

"It wasn't my fault," Cornelia protested. "I thought when I married him that James had bushels of money. I'd never have married him otherwise."

"We're getting lovely doses of truth," Emily said. "McNulty, would you have an extra stick of gum?" McNulty obliged.

"I knew that," James admitted. "I knew she didn't care about me, but I wanted her anyway. I had a comfortable income but with Cornelia that was never enough. I thought of this way of collecting a sizable sum from a group of people—no great hardship on any one of them, I was careful to see to that. In one case I reimbursed a fellow when I found he couldn't afford the loss. I wrote letters to these people, asking them to wire me whatever I thought they could afford for this mine I had rediscovered. I said I was investing heavily myself, and I wanted them to be in on it."

"Your ironclad respectability and conservatism, up to that point, fooled them. How did you collect the money without giving yourself away?" Burgreen inquired. "We got descriptions, but they didn't fit you."

"I had them wire the money to a bank—I didn't want my endorsement going back to them on checks. To collect when the money arrived I used my own identification papers, of course, but I disguised my appearance slightly—Hollywood shirt, plaid jacket, dark glasses, a beard." James smiled ruefully. "I was a horrible sight, really."

"That was the description we got," Burgreen said. "And since there are about five thousand such characters entering Las Vegas from California every month we were exactly nowhere."

"What was Cornelia doing while all this went on?" Emily wanted to know.

Cornelia looked uncomfortable, and Burgreen supplied the answer. "Mrs. Lord was rather busy at the time with a character named Donald Clark. Plenty of money, and very flashy. Wouldn't be surprised if he gave Lord the idea—"

"Not the idea," James corrected. "Shall we say the impetus? I confess I was frightfully jealous of that fellow."

"So you used his name as a red herring when you planted the letter in Mrs. Delaphine's desk, saying that a Donald Clark would call on her the night of the thirteenth," Henry said. "The other red herring was Beardsley Satchel. How did you manage to get red paint on his overcoat?"

"Satchel doesn't watch his overcoat or anything else when he gets in Charley's bar," James reminded him. "I couldn't hope that Satchel would be found guilty, still I did what I could to mislead the police and to throw suspicion on unpleasant persons."

"What put you on the right track?" Link asked Burgreen.

"Bailey and Rousseau of Boston. Nobody could have chosen a more ineffectual pair of detectives. He didn't want them to find out anything. Why? Because he had pulled the swindle himself."

Cornelia observed that James had been very stupid about the whole thing. "You could have made Cleo's death look like suicide," she said, "and no one would have been surprised. She was extremely erratic and very unhappy about losing Harmon."

"Unfortunately I killed her with your gun, my dear. I couldn't leave that on the scene and have it traced to you. I didn't mean to kill her at all—the idea hadn't even occurred to me. I took the gun as a threat, but Cleo got me so worked up that I didn't know what I was doing. She seemed determined to ruin me."

"Perhaps she didn't believe the money was all gone," Henry suggested.

"No, she didn't," James said. "She told me she would call the district attorney. In fact she picked up the phone—"

"That's why the phone was on the floor," Burgreen interrupted.

"Cleo could be somewhat exasperating," James explained.

Link snorted. "I nearly brained her with a candelabra myself."

"What about all the buzzing around in Cleo's house after the murder?" Henry asked. "How did you plant the letter from this Donald Clark?"

James said he had done that the night he killed her. "I didn't dare remain in her house long enough, at that time, to hunt for the letter she was going to use to expose me. I did go through the house quite carefully the night Mr. Ford died. When I saw the cape on Emily, though, and found how she had obtained it, I was certain Cleo had hidden the letter in that. It wasn't like her to refrain from mink."

"How did Harmon get the little Italian box?" Emily wondered.

Burgreen said he had probably picked it up while he was in the house the morning after the murder. "Of course with McNulty on the scene, nothing like that could possibly happen."

"I didn't see him touch nothing," McNulty said plaintively. "But you can't see everything, with the place full of cops and reporters and guys from the examiner's office. She was the kind of a stiff that brings a crowd."

Link turned to James. "I could forgive you for doing away with Delaphine, but when it comes to this ghastly business with the clams, and a plan to destroy our Emily, I don't even want to be in the same country with you."

"Were you going to kill me last night in the Long Island station, James?" Emily asked.

He looked puzzled. "I wasn't in the Long Island station."

"Who followed me home in a taxi, then?"

"I did," Link said. "I wanted you to get there in one piece."

"Then nobody was haunting me in the station?"

"Nobody," Link said. "You were pretty nervous, you know."

Burgreen knocked the ashes out of his pipe into a tin bucket, wrapped the clams in a paper. "Let's go, McNulty. If you're ready, Mr. Lord."

Cornelia had a frightened look, and Henry felt a little sorry for his sister, even though the whole thing was in a sense her fault. He asked Link to take her home. "Come back and meet us in Gottlieb's and we'll have dinner together."

"A few clams?" Link asked, leading Cornelia away.

Emily began to cry. "I feel awful," she said.

"You might feel a lot worse." Henry put his arms around her, kissed her damp and somewhat grimy face. "I hate to say this, Emily, but I'm afraid I'm going to marry you."

Emily felt in her pockets for Kleenex, and he gave her a handkerchief. "You're not just saying that to make me feel better?"

"No. Damn it, I love you, Emily."

"When did you find out?"

"In Lord & Taylor's. When I realized you might be dead when I got here, I felt awful."

The door opened and Roscoe came in carrying a brown-and-white puppy. "Merry Christmas, boss!" he said, handing the puppy to Emily.

"Isn't he darling! Is he for me, Roscoe?"

"Sure. I know you like him. I see many dogs in Gimbel's, but I think you need more a small dog for the apartment."

"You're sweet, Roscoe. What kind is he?"

"Saint Bernard," Henry told her.

They all went over to Gottlieb's and Mr. Gottlieb admired the puppy. "A friend?" he inquired.

"He's mine," Emily told him. "His name is Eve—for Christmas. Honestly, this is the nicest Christmas I've ever had. Henry is going to marry me. I did it with clams."

"Good," Mr. Gottlieb said. "I go order your dinner."

Link came along and sat down, and Emily told him the news. "I knew it would happen sooner or later," he said, "but I didn't think it would take two murders to do it. Emily, how in the world did you know James was the murderer?"

Roscoe said Miss Murdock was a very smart woman.

"Thank you, Roscoe," Emily said. "But I didn't know. I thought Henry killed them."

"You thought I did it?" Henry stared.

"It was just logic, Henry. It came to me all at once, while I was sitting on the edge of my bed. That's why I went to Babylon last night, I had to tell somebody, so I told my mother."

"What did she say?" Henry inquired.

"She wasn't surprised. She said she always thought you took a silver tablespoon the time she asked you out for Thanksgiving dinner."

THE END

About the Rue Morgue Press

"Rue Morgue Press is the old-mystery lover's best friend, reprinting high quality books from the 1930s and '40s."
—*Ellery Queen's Mystery Magazine*

Since 1997, the Rue Morgue Press has reprinted scores of traditional mysteries, the kind of books that were the hallmark of the Golden Age of detective fiction. Authors reprinted or to be reprinted by the Rue Morgue include Dorothy Bowers, Joanna Cannan, Glyn Carr, Torrey Chanslor, Clyde B. Clason, Joan Coggin, Manning Coles, Lucy Cores, Frances Crane, Norbert Davis, Elizabeth Dean, Constance & Gwenyth Little, Marlys Millhiser, James Norman, Stuart Palmer, Craig Rice, Kelley Roos, Charlotte Murray Russell, Maureen Sarsfield, and Juanita Sheridan.

To suggest titles or to receive a catalog of Rue Morgue Press books write P.O. Box 4119, Boulder, CO 80306, telephone 800-699-6214, or check out our website, www.ruemorguepress.com, which lists complete descriptions of all of our titles, along with lengthy biographies of our writers.